THE LIBRARY

Zoran Živković

THE LIBRARY

Zoran Živković

Translated from the Serbian by
Alice Copple-Tošić

Kurodahan Press

The Library
Zoran Živković

Translated from the Serbian by Alice Copple-Tošić

Copyright © 2002 Zoran Živković

FG-RS0004-L29

ISBN-13: 978-4-902075-33-5

KURODAHAN PRESS

Kurodahan Press is a division of Intercom, Ltd.

#403 Tenjin 3-9-10, Chuo-ku, Fukuoka 810-0001 JAPAN

www.kurodahan.com

To Mike Moorcock, a good man

Contents

1. Virtual Library

Email isn't perfect. Although Internet providers probably do their best to protect us from receiving unwanted messages, there seems to be no remedy against it. Whenever I open up the in-box on my screen, I almost always find at least one from an unknown sender. Usually there are several; the record was thirteen junk mail messages, sent over just a few hours, in between two sessions at the computer.

When that happened I really got irritated and changed my e-address, despite considerable inconvenience. I gave out my new address only to a small number of people, but to no avail. The pesky emails soon began arriving once again. I complained to my provider, who admitted in a roundabout way that they could do nothing to help. They advised me just to delete everything that didn't interest me, particularly since dangerous computer viruses often spread through junk mail.

The recommendation was unnecessary as I had already been deleting my junk mail, even though I was unaware of the viruses. At first, I'd read these messages in bewilderment, but once I realized what was going on, I deleted every e-message of unknown origin without delay. I didn't even give them a cursory reading, despite the fact that the senders took all kinds of pains to attract my attention. Bombastic, flickering headings with fancy, ostentatious illustrations advertised a variety of exceptional offers not to be missed at any cost.

One proposal, for example, would make me rich overnight if I invested money through a glamorous-sounding agency from some Pacific Rim country I had never heard of. Or, after a two-week correspondence course, I could become a preacher in any Christian church I wanted, authorized to carry out baptismal, wedding, and funeral rites. I also had the opportunity, regardless of my age, to turn back the clock twenty-five years using some new macrobiotic remedy. I was offered the unique opportunity, for a modest commission of forty-nine percent, finally to get hold of the money that had been awarded me by the court, if I had any such claims. I could also satisfy my assumed passion for gambling at any hour of the day or night, playing in some virtual casino guaranteed to be honest. Lastly, to top it all off, I was offered at a mere pittance, under the counter, two and a half million verified, active e-addresses to which I could send whatever I wanted as many times as I wanted.

Perhaps the email that started it all would have ended up in the recycle bin along with the others, if it had not been so brief that I inadvertently read it. Against a black background, devoid of decoration, the first line announced: VIRTUAL LIBRARY in large, yellow letters, while under it the slogan "We have everything!"—written in considerably smaller blue letters—did not exactly assume the aggressive tone typical of this type of message.

Of all the exaggeration I had come across on the Internet, this one took the biscuit. Really, "everything!" Such a claim would be absurd even for web sites from the largest world libraries. Whoever had come up with this scheme certainly had no notion just how many books have been published in the last five thousand years. No one has ever managed to put such a library together in one place, even discounting all those works that have disappeared into oblivion.

And then there was that word "virtual." Used in its truest sense, "virtual" should mean a library composed of electronic books. The Internet has several sites containing such e-editions and I visit them from time to time. But they offer slim pickings. Only several hundred titles are available, just

3

a drop in the ocean compared to "everything" in the literal sense. Who would even dare to hope that this vast multitude could ever be transferred into computer form? And who would ever find it worth the effort?

Although I was convinced this must be a hoax, my curiosity stopped me from proceeding as usual. If it had involved anything other than books, I would have ignored the message without a second thought. But for a writer this was like waving a red flag in front of a bull. Instead of deleting the message, I positioned the cursor on the text. The arrow turned into a hand with a raised index finger and I found myself at the Virtual Library site.

The change was barely noticeable. The background stayed black, with two small additions appearing under the name of the site and the slogan. The first was the standard search field: a narrow white rectangular space in which to type the search text. This, however, could not be the title of a work or some other data, since the word "Author" appeared at the beginning. I shook my head. More sophisticated capabilities were to be expected from a library that prided itself on being the "ultimate." At the very bottom of the screen was a short e-address.

I typed in my own name. This was not out of vanity, although it might have appeared so. I chose myself because, obviously, I am most familiar with my own work. If the Virtual Library truly contained what it claimed in its slogan, then my three books should be no exception. I am certainly not a well-known or popular writer, but I still should be included in a library containing all authors. In such a place there should be no discrimination of any kind.

There were two possible outcomes. If the search did not produce the expected result, which was quite likely, then the whole thing was probably a practical joke. Someone had decided to have some fun at the expense of writers, or perhaps publishers, critics, librarians, bookshop owners, and the book world in general. Who knew what kind of trick might be played instead of a page listing my works. But I had no right to complain; no one had forced me to visit the site. A joke would serve me right for not minding my own business.

If, however, my books appeared in electronic form, then the situation was considerably worse. I had not ceded my rights to anyone for such publication, which would mean they were pirated editions. That really would be a problem. The Internet is awash with this type of abuse, and as far as I have heard, protection from it is just as difficult as protection from unwanted e-messages.

If my work did exist in the Virtual Library, the search would have to last some time. Regardless of increases in computer speed, the gigantic corpus involved could certainly not be searched in a moment. But that is just what happened. As soon as I clicked the mouse to begin the search, a new page appeared on the screen. This time it had a gray background, with black and white writing. A smaller picture also appeared in color, disturbing the uniformity.

At first I thought that the speed with which it had been found was a sure sign of something fishy. But when I found myself squinting at my own face on the screen, a shudder ran down my spine. That was me, no doubt about it, although I had no idea when and where the picture had been taken. I appeared to be somewhat younger, but it was hard to tell how much younger.

Under the picture, on the left-hand side of the screen, I found a brief biography. All the information was correct, except for the last bit. Unless something had happened without my noticing it, I was still very much alive. The facts about my death, though, were strangely undefined. The word "died" was followed by nine different years, separated by commas. Unlike the black letters before them, these numbers were white. The closest year was a decade and a half in the future, while the most distant was almost half a century away. Whoever had edited the entry obviously had a morbid sense of humor.

On the right-hand side of the screen I found a list of my books. It did not end, however, after the third book. It continued all the way to number twenty-one which, of course, was ridiculous. I'm not saying that such a voluminous bibliography didn't please me, but it simply was not mine. Two colors had been used here as well. The three books I had actually published appeared in black type, while the other eighteen works appeared in white. These other titles were presented in chronological order. The first dated from the following year, and there were forty-five years to go until the last date. So I was dealing not only with a twisted prankster, but someone who seemed to imagine himself a clairvoyant.

None of this mattered, however; I still had to find out the most important thing. Was this just the work of some idler who had nothing better to do than fool around with such nonsense? The Internet is full of people who think nothing of putting time and effort into pulling off stunts like this. Hackers are a good example. They invent and spread destructive viruses, even though they gain no benefit other than an insular satisfaction. I clicked the cursor on the first of my three books, certain that nothing would happen. But the arrow, unfortunately, turned into a hand again and the screen soon filled with text.

I had only to read the first sentence to confirm that this really was my first novel. A wave of anger rolled over me. My book was accessible to the whole world without any permission or payment! How dared they! Why, this was highway robbery! And then suddenly I was filled with the hope that perhaps it wasn't all there, that maybe only an excerpt had been posted, which might be somewhat bearable. But as soon as I scrolled down to the end of the page, I lost this faint hope. The whole book was there, from the first word to the last. I didn't even have to open the other two titles. I knew perfectly well what I would find.

Enraged, I reached for the mouse once more, clicked on the button, and returned to the previous page. I brought the cursor to the e-address at the bottom, then clicked again. My browser opened a blank email window with the site's email address in the "To" field. I stared at the empty page for a few moments, deliberating. Finally, I wrote "Piracy" in the "Subject" line, then started to write.

Dear Sir,

A very unpleasant surprise awaited me when I visited the Virtual Library site. I found my three novels there freely accessible to anyone. Since I, as the copyright holder, never gave permission for such publication, it clearly represents an act of publishing piracy, punishable by law. I order you to withdraw my works from your site without delay. I would also like to inform you that my lawyer will soon be sending you a request for due compensation for damages, not only for the unauthorized placement of my books on your site but also for the inaccurate, and insulting, additions to my biography and bibliography.

The Library

I signed my name at the end, without any closing salutation. It was impolite, but I couldn't think of anything that sounded appropriate. It would have been hard to put the formal "sincerely yours" or "yours truly." I also had trouble adopting a suitably severe tone for my missive; I had no experience of this sort of thing. The letter, I suppose, must have appeared harsh enough and a warning, although, to tell the truth, I did not count on it having much effect. The most that could be expected was for them to remove the page containing my works, while I hadn't the slightest hope of receiving any compensation.

I even doubted that I would receive a reply. But I was mistaken. Just after I sent the email, a message came back in response. The only explanation was that the editors of the Virtual Library, flooded with similar protest letters, had a ready-made reply to be sent automatically upon receipt of such a complaint. They probably didn't receive any other kind of letter. What did they have to say in their defense?

Highly esteemed sir,

First, please allow us to express our deepest gratitude to you for having shown us the honor of visiting the Virtual Library.

We hasten to dispel your fears. This is not an unauthorized publication of your works. Although the page devoted to you does contain the texts of your books, access to that page is not at all free, as you have assumed. It is allowed exclusively to you, and only once. Since you have just used this opportunity, you may rest assured that no one will ever again be able to access the page containing your bio-bibliography. You will see this for yourself should you try to return to it.

Regarding the information that you have concluded is incorrect, please rest assured that it is accurate.

Sincerely yours,

Virtual Library

So they had it all worked out. As soon as an author complained, they quickly removed the page. No page, no proof of piracy. I had nonetheless expected something more ingenious. That page still existed in the "cache" memory of my computer as irrefutable proof. All I had to do was hit the "Back" button and save it. Nothing easier. In addition, it seemed the Virtual Library considered writers to be so computer illiterate and naive that they would easily swallow the story about access to their page. Nonsense. As if something like that were even possible. Or that bit about the accuracy of the invented data. What a misjudgment.

I quickly clicked "Back" on the toolbar. But something unexpected happened. Instead of showing the previous page, the window with the letter from the Virtual Library closed, and the

"Back" button became inactive, as though nothing had been stored in the "cache" file. I stared in bewilderment at the primarily black picture on the screen, uncomprehending. The page had to be there. I had been on it just a few minutes before and had done nothing in the meantime to delete it.

Obviously, something had gone wrong. I wasn't computer illiterate, but I also was not skilled enough to figure out everything that could go wrong with these strange machines. But it made no difference, I would enter my name once again in the search rectangle. Although I had been informed that access to my page would henceforth be blocked, it would be hard for them to do so instantaneously. Unfortunately, the search came up blank this time. The program informed me that no writer with my name could be found in the library that included all authors who had ever existed.

Confusion and anger started to get the upper hand. I looked like a fool who, thanks to his own rashness, had been taken in by a cheap trick. It even crossed my mind that a throng of happy people from some television station might burst into my study at any moment, revealing that all of this had been just a cleverly organized candid camera episode. But no one appeared and, after several long minutes, I did the only thing I could do. I clicked once again on the lower e-address and started to type a new email.

Dear Sir,

I don't know how you did it, but that's not important. Your joke—I could use a stronger word—is tasteless to say the least. People like you are inflicting enormous damage on the noble idea of the Internet. You should be ashamed of yourselves. Don't forget that I still have the address of your web site. I will try to trace you through it. Your library might be virtual, but you certainly are not.

Once again I used my signature, without any closing formality. Good manners were superfluous to the situation. I should have left out the "Dear Sir" too. The people behind this travesty did not deserve such a courtesy. When I sent the message I was again sure there would be no reply. How could they respond to my accusation? But I got one anyway, at the same instant, just like before. The speed of the reply should have aroused my suspicions, of course, since this letter could not have been prepared in advance like the previous one. All caught up in my anger, I did not give proper consideration to this impossibility which was, in any case, not the first one I had encountered at the Virtual Library. How strange it is, the way one so easily starts to accept things that have no explanation, particularly when computers are involved.

Highly esteemed sir,

We are sorry that you received the wrong impression. Making jokes is the farthest thing from our intent. All our efforts go towards the serious execution of our responsible work, which is the only fitting thing to do.

Sincerely yours,

Virtual Library

As I opened the window for a new letter to my unknown adversary, a sober voice inside tried to dissuade me. It was pointless taking any more part in such a farce. I had already achieved as much as I could, given the circumstances. The page with my works had been removed and further correspondence would lead nowhere. Unfortunately, one does not always listen to sober advice.

I suppose you expect me to take the list of books cited as mine seriously, even though they have not yet been written. I might have admired your ability to foretell the future if you had not been so indecisive regarding the year of my death. Nine possibilities! I would appreciate being informed when you decide on one of them. Timely knowledge in this regard would considerably facilitate the remainder of my life, however long it might be.

This time I even omitted my signature. That fact, and the conspicuously sarcastic tone of the letter, should have indicated what I thought of them, had they been previously unaware. Their pointed politeness, not at all appropriate to the circumstances, had started to get on my nerves. The answer arrived once again a moment after I sent my message, but this no longer amazed me. Sleights-of-hand cease to be interesting when they are repeated too often, even if you don't know how they are performed.

Highly esteemed sir,

We are unfortunately unable to inform you of when you will die. It is not easy to forecast the future. All nine possibilities have equal footing at this moment. Chance will decide which of them comes true. Your bibliography contains all the works from all these futures. However, you will not write and publish all eighteen of them on a single one of the branches of life that await you, to use a picturesque expression. Your later works will include at most eleven and at least six books. You were only able to see them all on our site. We therefore hope that we have justified our slogan.

Sincerely yours,

Virtual Library

Just as I finished reading the message, it vanished, the window in which it was located suddenly closing even though I had not touched any keys. A moment later, the same thing happened to the browser window. The only window left open was for email, but it did not contain the original message from the Virtual Library, although it should have been there, since I had not deleted it. Before I closed it, I checked to see if any new email messages had arrived in the meantime, but there were none.

I sat there for a long time, eyes unfocussed, staring at the empty screen before me. I did not try to understand. The ways of the computer are often incomprehensible to me. I searched my memory, but hard as I tried the text written in white against a gray background to the right of my photograph did not become sharp enough to read. It seemed to be covered by a shimmering, impenetrable veil. Finally, even though frustration weighed me down, I abandoned my vain efforts and turned off the computer.

From then on, I continued to delete unwanted email messages, but no longer right away. First I read them, even when it was immediately apparent that they did not deserve the slightest attention. I felt foolish as I skimmed through various incoherent offers, particularly since I hadn't the faintest hope of ever seeing among them one that was quite brief, on a black background. But such was the burden I had to bear.

2. Home Library

I unlocked the mailbox.

All I ever found in it were bills at the beginning of the month, but I still checked it regularly when I returned from work. I checked it on Saturday and Sunday, too, at the same time as on the other days, even though the postman didn't deliver on those days. Just in case. In addition, on Tuesday I always took a handkerchief and wiped out the dust that had collected inside, although you couldn't see the dust from the outside. We have to take care of such places, perhaps even more than those that are visible to the eye. People tend to neglect them, even though they are actually the best testimony to meticulousness.

There should not have been anything in my mailbox because it was only the middle of the month. But when I opened the wooden door, I saw a large book, hardcover bound in dark yellow. It almost filled the entire mailbox. In my place somebody else would probably have found many reasons to be surprised by this sudden apparition. First of all, who had sent it to me? No one had ever sent me a book before. Why would anyone, anyhow? Plus, it wasn't even wrapped, and nothing on it indicated it was intended for me. So why had the postman put it in my mailbox? And finally, how had he managed to fit it inside? The book was a lot thicker than the narrow slit through which he inserted bills. It certainly could not have got in through the slit.

I, however, wasn't surprised at all. I didn't let any of these annoying questions upset me. Long ago, I realized that the world is full of inexplicable wonders. It's no use even trying to explain them. Those who try anyway just end up unhappy. And why should a person be unhappy when he doesn't have to be? Unusual things should be accepted for what they are, without explanation. That is the easiest way to live with them.

Before this became clear to me, various unaccountable phenomena had made my life miserable. For example, the number of steps between my second-floor apartment and the ground floor. I'm used to counting steps, half out loud, everywhere and on all occasions, even when I already know the number of steps. When I climb up to my apartment, there are always forty-four steps.

The Library

Whenever I walk down to the ground floor, there are only forty-one. For a while after I moved here, I found myself in some discomfort because of this difference. I tried just about everything to figure out what was wrong.

I first attempted to outsmart the stairs. I counted them to myself while keeping my mouth firmly shut, so there was no way of knowing what I was up to. It didn't work. On the way up there were still persistently three more steps than on the way down. Then I counted them while walking backwards; although I walked carefully, this was not only difficult and dangerous, but for some reason also drew confused and suspicious looks from my neighbors. Despite my greeting them politely, raising my hat and nodding, they would just mumble in reply with their heads down. People can really act oddly sometimes.

Finally, it occurred to me to count the steps in the dark. I would leave the apartment after midnight wearing light, rubber-soled shoes so my footsteps wouldn't wake anyone. Without turning on the light in the stairwell, I walked down to the ground floor, then climbed back up to my apartment, down and up, up and down, until dawn. It wasn't hard, despite the murky darkness, because I knew the exact number of steps in either direction. I would have had a hard time—stairs can be dangerous even when you can see quite well, let alone in the pitch black of night like that—if I had stuck to what common sense told me: that the number of steps must be the same going up and coming down.

That's when I gave up trying to find an explanation for everything no matter what the cost. Common sense is all very well and good, but you can't always rely on it. Sometimes it is far more advisable and useful to accept a wonder. It might even save your neck, and that's no small thing. Not only did I survive the dark stairwell, I quickly regained my peace of mind. As soon as I stopped burdening myself with superfluous curiosity, I slept better, my appetite returned, and I wasn't chronically depressed, apathetic and anemic any longer. It's amazing how one simple decision can make a new man out of you in no time at all.

So now, instead of wasting time being amazed, I took the book out of my mailbox and examined it. The title was written in large, ornate black letters: *World Literature*. There were no other words on the cover, not even the author's name. I was not surprised, for how could anyone truly be the writer of such a work? I quickly leafed through the book and discovered there were even more pages than the size indicated because the paper was very thin, like onionskin. This suited the title: anything more limited in scope would hardly fit the bill. The edition seemed quite splendid in all respects. It even had a brown ribbon to mark your place when you had stopped reading.

The Library

I put *World Literature* under my arm and headed up to my apartment. I reached the twentieth step, then stopped short. Today was Tuesday! That fact had slipped my mind owing to the unexpected appearance of the book. I had no choice but to walk back down. One should not let anything interfere with carrying out one's duties, not even an unforeseen event. Descending to the ground floor, I took from the inside pocket of my jacket the green silk handkerchief used exclusively to clean the mailbox.

When I opened it, another surprise awaited me: another thick, dark yellow book with the same title. Someone unaccustomed to wonders would probably have been flabbergasted. Such a person might have stepped back, heart racing, a shudder running down his spine. Once he had collected his wits, he would begin feverishly searching for an explanation, but it would be hard to come up with anything coherent. I hesitate to think of what he might do afterwards. Maybe even attempt suicide.

But I, of course, remained perfectly calm. There was no reason to get upset. I simply took out the second volume of *World Literature*, put it under my arm with the other one, and wiped out the mailbox. I only needed one hand for that, thank goodness. As usual, I concentrated on the lower corners, from which it was hardest to remove the dust and yet where it most collected, as if out of spite.

I locked the mailbox door once again and headed for the second floor. This time I did not get very far: I'd just raised my foot to the first step when a thought struck me and brought me back to the mailbox. As I opened it, a surge of excitement flowed through me. Everyone enjoys having premonitions come true, particularly if they are auspicious. Had one of my neighbors walked by at that moment, he would have seen my face light up when a third dark yellow book appeared behind the door.

I can't explain how I suspected it would be there. Intuition, I guess, but not only that. Such an idea would never occur to a person who was hostile to wonders. That's another advantage of not giving in to prejudice. I took the new *World Literature*, but didn't put it under my arm. I couldn't hold three thick volumes. Instead, I placed the books in the crook of my left arm. Then I locked the door again, but this time I waited in front of the mailbox. I stood there for several moments, trying not to appear too impatient, then opened the mailbox a fourth time. Even though glad to see it filled once again, I found my previous excitement was somehow missing. Self-satisfaction is in bad taste. Or at least, showing it openly is.

After the thirteenth book I had to stop, mostly because of the weight. In my fervor, I'd forgotten that books, contrary to popular belief, are not light, particularly when gathered in a pile. They had to be carried up to the second floor. I certainly would have had an easier time taking them down the stairs rather than climbing up, because, inter alia, there were three fewer steps going down. In addition, the load turned out to be quite awkward. I had to stretch my arms almost to my knees in order to hold the books piled one on top of the other, while my chin on top secured this unstable arrangement, with my head forced back. I looked around uneasily. It wouldn't be good for one of my neighbors to see me carrying too many of the same kind of book. Who knew what they might think? People have a tendency to jump to conclusions.

When I finally got home, I was gasping for breath. I had a hard time unlocking the three locks, the armload of books briefly supported by just one hand. The bottom lock, next to the threshold, gave me particular difficulty. I had to squat, barely keeping my balance. If any other title had been involved, I might have had to put them down on the floor. Because I fastidiously clean the area around my front door, the books would not have gotten dirty, but the thought of *World Literature* against cold tile seemed somehow improper. Almost a sacrilege.

Once I entered the apartment, I was confronted by the problem of where to put the books. I hesitated and stood next to the door for a time, not knowing what to do with them. In the end, I put them on the table until I could give it some more thought. The best solution would have been a bookshelf. That's the right place for books. Unfortunately, I didn't have one. What did I need a bookshelf for when I didn't own any books?

Since moving to the apartment, I had not kept a home library. My apartment is small—just a studio. One little room, a vestibule, a kitchenette and a bathroom. You can't even turn around without banging your arms against the walls. And it is a well-known fact that books devour space. You can't reverse this law. However much space you give them, it's never enough. First they occupy the walls. Then they continue to spread wherever they can gain a foothold. Only ceilings are spared the invasion. New books keep arriving, and you can't bear to get rid of a single old one. And so, slowly and imperceptibly, the volumes crowd out everything before them. Like glaciers.

But now I had no choice. The books were already in my apartment and they had to be put somewhere. I couldn't just leave them in the mailbox. After all, I'm a mature, responsible man. How would it look if I pretended, ostrich-like, that they weren't there? If nothing else, inaction on my part would arouse the postman's suspicions the next time he tried to insert my bills and couldn't because the mailbox was full. He would wonder why I hadn't picked up my mail. He might even come up to ask me about it. And what could I tell him?

The Library

No, ignoring the books was out of the question. I had to bring them into the apartment. Later I would figure out what to do with them.

Now the question became how to carry up the rest of them, assuming there were more. I couldn't do what I had done the first time. That was too inconvenient. I had to find something suitable in which to carry the books. Looking around the room, I finally remembered something that would suit the purpose, although it was not within my field of vision. I took a large suitcase with brass reinforcements on the corners out of the double-fronted wardrobe. I could fit lots of books inside, which was all to the good. However, once filled, it would be extremely heavy. Sometimes you can't have your cake and eat it too.

Bringing up fifty-six volumes of *World Literature* all at once to the second floor was no easy matter. I had to hold the suitcase handle with both hands. On the twenty-eighth step, I realized I shouldn't have loaded myself down so much. However, if I'd taken fewer books, I would have had to make the climb several times, actually gaining nothing. Only an elevator would have made any difference, but unfortunately the building didn't have one. Not a single shortcut could be taken if I wanted to bring the books up to my apartment.

While I started to take out the books and put them next to the first thirteen, I realized I had another problem. One more full suitcase and the thin legs of the little table would give way under the weight. And then what? Before continuing, I had to devise a plan. Something like this couldn't be approached haphazardly. I had no idea how many more volumes would appear in my mailbox. Maybe just a few, maybe hundreds. Most likely the latter. This was world literature, after all, and had to be enormous, even when printed on onionskin. I had to prepare for the worst.

The furniture in my only room was sparse, which now turned out to be a blessing. Along with the table and wardrobe, I had four chairs, a bed, a dresser and a night table. I pushed them all into a corner, freeing up about two-thirds of the available space. Naturally, this had an equal and opposite effect: the area to the right of the door was now cramped and crowded. That didn't bother me. Exceptional circumstances require a man to make sacrifices without complaint. Besides, I had never cared much for comfort.

I spread newspapers across the floor in the empty part of the room. It was spotlessly clean, of course, but this way seemed more appropriate. Then I started to move the books. This required some planning. I began by arranging them in the corner farthest from the door—the same place I would have started if polishing the floor, for example. A stack of exactly forty volumes fitted from floor to ceiling. In order to place the last seven, I had to climb onto a chair. The tall yellow column would probably have toppled if it hadn't been leaning against two walls and secured firmly from above by the last book that I barely managed to wedge in. I got down from the chair, took a step back and admired the scene.

With my strategy established, all I had to do was get down to work. There could be no hesitation. Who knew how long the whole thing would last? I took the empty suitcase and headed downstairs. I had simplified the operation, so now I could act more quickly. After taking one volume out of the mailbox, I would just close the door briefly and then open it again. I didn't need to lock and unlock it. A new volume was already waiting inside. I became skilled at arranging the books in the suitcase, managing to fit in fifty-eight volumes.

My neighbors passed by several times, but no one paid any attention to me. All they did was look away and quicken their steps. It's hard to understand people sometimes. I don't mean to suggest that this lack of interest didn't suit me— I didn't want to explain my actions, even though in point of fact I didn't have to answer to anyone for them—but such indifference was nonetheless inexcusable. What if someone with suspicious intent, or even worse with questionable sanity, had been there in my place? These days, all kinds of disturbed people loiter around respectable apartment complexes.

As time passed, exhaustion inevitably crept over me. After the twenty-seventh suitcase, I could no longer reach the second floor without a short break. The most logical idea was to take a break in the middle, after the twenty-second step, particularly since it was on the first floor. But I ran into trouble after the forty-ninth suitcase, at which time I decided to take a second break. Forty-four steps cannot be evenly divided into three parts. I was forced to resort to an inelegant solution. The first time, I stopped briefly after the fifteenth step, the second time after the thirtieth, with only fourteen steps left in the third part of my journey. The dissonance of the solution bothered me until the sixty-third suitcase, when the need arose for one more rest. Forty-four is divisible by four, thank heavens, so I was able to stop after every eleventh step, i.e., on the landings and on the first floor.

When I brought up the ninety-second suitcase, its contents filled the area I had emptied. Before me rose an enormous dark yellow wall. To behold world literature in this way revealed its true majesty. Night had fallen long ago, but I was still surprised when I looked at the clock and realized it was 2:17 a.m.

I could work deep into the night without bothering my neighbors because I didn't have to turn on the light in the stairwell. I also took special pains to be as quiet as possible. I even took off my shoes. The entrance to the bathroom, where I kept my lightweight shoes, was blocked by piles, so I stayed in my socks, but thanks to the warm weather I was in no danger of catching cold. I probably should have changed into something more appropriate, but in my rush I failed to do so. All the hauling had completely wrinkled the suit I wore to work, my shirt was soaked in sweat and my tie was loose. At least I had taken off my hat.

An end to my torment, however, did not seem likely. Regardless of how many times I emptied the mailbox, it was full the next time I opened the door. I had no other choice but to find space for the new books. I hesitated several moments about which piece of furniture I could best do without. I finally decided on the bed because it almost certainly would not be needed that night. I would have trouble finding time to take even the shortest break. Although small, the bed was heavy. As I carried it down, I was consoled by the thought that it would have been much heavier carried in the opposite direction. I took it to my basement storage space. The space was small but empty because I had nothing to store inside it. I pulled the bed upright, anticipating that sooner or later I would have to put something else inside as well.

Shortly before 5:00 a.m., after the one hundred and nineteenth suitcase, my fears became reality. The space vacated by the bed was now filled to the ceiling with dark yellow volumes. I agonized over what to take to the basement next, and then realized that it didn't matter. There was no sense in fooling myself. Each piece of furniture would have to be removed in its turn, so the best thing was to take it all at once. Now was the right time, while everyone slept. It could be done inconspicuously and not under the inquisitive gaze of the neighbors.

I had no trouble moving the table, chairs, dresser and night table, but the wardrobe gave me a real headache. Not just because it was heavy, but because of its bulk. I staggered and swerved underneath it, struggling to keep my balance. On two occasions I almost fell. I carried it on my back most of the time, trying to make as little noise as possible, although I couldn't help some squeaking and cracking. With luck, I hadn't woken anyone up. In any case, no one came out to see what was going on.

Once I reached the basement, all my efforts almost went for naught. It took considerable ingenuity and maneuvering to get the wardrobe through the narrow door. Not only was my storage compartment crammed, but I didn't see how anything could be removed without breaking down the partition wall.

As dawn approached, the rest of the free space in the room filled up. Before blocking the bathroom entrance with books, I spent several minutes inside. It was either then or never. I came out a bit more refreshed and tidy. I hadn't been able to re-move all the traces of the night's hard work, but I hoped I wouldn't look too shocking when I began to meet my neighbors in the stairwell. In order to improve the impression I made, I put on my hat and shoes.

When it came time to cover the door to the kitchenette with books, I thought I might take at least the refrigerator and little stove out of there, if not the dishes and cutlery. But I had to abandon that idea. I didn't know what to do with those bulky items. There wasn't any room left in the basement and I couldn't leave them by the front door. No, they could stay inside; even though in-accessible, they weren't in the way.

At 8:26 a.m., after the one hundred and forty-third suitcase, I had finally packed the room. Eight thousand three hundred and five books! It was truly an impressive sight; after wedging in the last volume, I stood in the solemn silence, looking on in admiration. Had anyone anywhere ever had a chance to see all of world literature crammed into such a small space? It left me breathless. The enormous effort had been worthwhile in the end.

I didn't have much time to admire the sight, however. I had to leave for work. In all my years on the job, I have never been late. I would be able to enjoy the books to my heart's content when I returned home in the afternoon. I would sit in the vestibule in front of the open door to the room and just stare at the dark yellow treasury before me. What else did a man need? A chair, perhaps? No, I didn't need a chair. My needs have always been modest. Since I'd already done away with all the other things, I would make do without a chair. In any case, I would not be sitting on the bare floor. I had a rug made of pure wool.

Descending to the ground floor, I unlocked the door to the mailbox once again. Even though it was only Wednesday, I took the green handkerchief and wiped the inside, although in my rush I was not as thorough as usual. Books are clean, particularly new ones, but after so many volumes passing through the mailbox, there must have been some dust left behind.

3. Night Library

I shouldn't have gone to the movie first. If I'd known it would last almost two hours, I'd have gone to the library beforehand. I might have felt silly with several books on my lap during the movie, but I doubt anyone would have noticed. As it was, around 7:30 p.m. I began to squirm in my seat. I kept turning my left wrist towards the screen so I could see my watch. Although gripping, the plot seemed more drawn out than it should have been. I was tempted to leave before the end, but since I was sitting in the middle of the row, it would have been too awkward.

When the movie finally ended at ten to eight, I hurried out of the theater. I received several reproachful glances and heard muffled complaints as, apologizing, I cut my way through the moviegoers who were closer to the exit. If I quickened my pace, I might still make it. The library was not far from the movie theater. It closed at eight, but I was a frequent visitor. I could probably count on bit of forbearance from the staff.

Everything would have been different, of course, if it hadn't been Friday. Saturday and Sunday, the library would be closed, meaning that if I failed, I would have nothing to read over the weekend, a possibility that wasn't at all pleasing. Since I live alone, I am inevitably faced with an abundance of free time that has to be filled somehow. Long ago I discovered that reading was much more useful and pleasant than dulling my senses in front of the television.

The threat of spending the next two days in front of the television, filled with frustration and self-reproach, forced me into a run. Running wasn't easy, however, because it had started to snow while I was at the movie. Driven by the wind, the large, thick flakes fell at a slant, hitting me in the face as I rushed forward. I finally had to open my umbrella, holding it in front of me to ward off the snow. This slowed me down since I couldn't see where I was going. Luckily, I knew the way and in such weather there weren't many people in the street.

I reached the library at three minutes after eight. Looking through the glass door, I read the time on the large clock hanging from the ceiling in the foyer. The lights were still on, but if the door was locked not even my close relationship with the librarians would be of any help. I grabbed the cold doorknob apprehensively and pushed. I couldn't help but sigh with relief when the door opened. I entered quickly, turned to shake off the snow coating my umbrella, and then closed the door behind me.

I spent a few moments in the foyer cleaning the snow from my hair and stamping my feet on the doormat to remove bits of slush. I also took out a handkerchief and wiped off the water streaming down my glasses. I put my umbrella in the brass stand next to the door, then rushed up the narrow staircase to the main library area.

It was quite warm in the building, causing my cold glasses to fog up as I climbed the stairs. When I entered the large room illuminated by fluorescent lights, I had to take them off again and wipe them. Even though I am extremely near-sighted, I could move forward as I wiped my glasses since there were no obstacles on the wide, dark-red carpet before me. The tables and chairs were to the left, next to the tall windows. Holding my glasses and handkerchief, I advanced with long strides towards the counter at the opposite side of the room. To the right rose shelves full of catalogues and various reference books which, owing to my blurred vision, looked like dark, overhanging masses.

I put on my glasses the moment I reached the counter. I had already thought of an apologetic excuse I could make for being late, one that, accompanied by a suitable smile, would put the librarian in a good mood. Unless ill-tempered by nature, people are usually obliging in such circumstances, even when they consider the request excessive—probably so they can take pride in their kindness afterwards. However, I had no one to give my excuses to. There was no one sitting behind the counter. Had my glasses been in place, I would have noticed this earlier.

I turned around in bewilderment. Perhaps, preoccupied with wiping my glasses, I had passed by the librarian without noticing him. But there was no one behind me; the long room was yawningly empty. There was actually little chance that we had passed each other. I might have missed him but he wouldn't have missed me, and the librarian would have been certain to address me. Hesitant, I turned towards the counter once again. Then I realized what had probably happened. Since no one was expected, the personnel had retired to some back room in anticipation of going home.

I coughed loudly, but no one appeared at the half-open side door that was the main entrance to the area behind the counter. The light was on in the room behind the door, but no sound came from that direction. "Good evening," I said, and waited a bit, then repeated it in a louder voice. Still no response. Silence reigned in the library.

The Library

As I stood there, not knowing what to do, the lights suddenly went out. All at once I was surrounded by darkness. The windows that had been dim rectangles a moment before were now the only source of light. Through them came the orange glow of the streetlights, muted by a coating of snow. As my eyes adjusted to the darkness, I looked around, trying to figure out what might have happened and having no easy time of it.

Then, from somewhere downstairs I heard a sharp metal sound, like a key turning in a lock. That same moment, I realized what was going on. The personnel did not have to go through the main room to reach the ground floor. As I had waited in front of the counter, they had reached the stairs some other way, or had taken the elevator. On their way out, they had turned off the building's power from the central switch. That was a reasonable precaution for an institution such as a library.

"Wait!" I shouted, running across the room. In the darkness the carpet became a straight, black strip, allowing me to move quickly even without light. But when I reached the stairs I had to slow down. It was considerably darker in the windowless foyer. The only bit of light came from the glass door at the entrance. I groped for the handrail on the right, grabbed hold of it and started downward, even though I was already too late. There was no one by the door.

Turning the doorknob and pushing brought anger this time, not relief. I was most angry at the librarians. How could they just lock up and leave, without checking whether anyone was still inside? True, I had entered after working hours, but even so. What if a thief had entered instead of me? The library security system clearly left much to be desired. But I was also to blame, quite honestly. I have never had a high opinion of people who leave everything to the last minute, and that is exactly what I had done in my haste. All because of a movie that I could have seen another time. In fact, nothing would have been lost if I'd never seen it at all.

Well, agonizing over it now wouldn't help. I had to devise a way to get out of the building. The thought of staying locked in the library until Monday morning made me shudder. That would not do at all, even though I certainly would not be bored surrounded by so many books. The heating might have been turned off with the power. The building might become colder and colder with each passing hour; they might find me frozen in two and a half days, in spite of my warm coat. There were other problems, too. I would not die of thirst—the restroom was probably in working order—but how could I survive sixty hours without food? And where would I sleep? I couldn't just sit and read the whole time. I shook my head, still holding onto the doorknob, as though expecting the door to budge. There had to be a solution.

What would I do if I really were a thief? A thief would not wait until Monday to be let out. What would someone like that do in my place? I thought about it for a moment, but everything that crossed my mind was either too violent, too dangerous, too hard to carry out, or required tools that I did not have at my disposal. All in all, it seemed I could not depend on any latent aptitude for thievery.

Then it dawned on me—a simple solution, but one a thief would never think of even in his dreams. All I had to do was return to the counter and use the phone there. Telephones work when the power is off. I would simply call the police and explain my predicament. They might think it was a crank call, but even if they didn't believe me right away, I would keep on calling until they checked on me. After that it would all be plain sailing. They would probably take me to the police station to make a statement. Even a run-in with the police was more acceptable than languishing in the library for two and a half days.

Stepping with care through the pitch black that engulfed me when I turned my back to the entrance, I mounted the stairs, my hand upon the rail. Even though I could see nothing, climbing was not difficult, particularly since I no longer had to hurry and everything would be better as soon as I reached the room. And it truly was better, but not just because of the meagre light that poured in through the windows. Although weak and dimmed by the green plastic shade, the desk lamp at the counter seemed strong as a floodlight to me.

I stopped at the entrance to the main room and stared straight ahead. How could that lamp work if the power had been turned off in the whole building? Maybe I had jumped to the wrong conclusion. On their way out, the librarians had probably just turned off the ceiling lights. There could be no other explanation. But even so, someone had to turn on the lamp. When I'd left the room, it had not been on, and no one in the library but me could have turned it off. Or was I wrong about this as well?

As if in answer to my question, the door leading to the back room opened wide and someone entered the area behind the counter. I was rather far away, but I managed to make out a tall, thin, middle-aged man in a dark suit. He headed for the librarian's chair and sat down in it, turning his attention to something in front of him. He did not raise his head towards me. Even if he had looked in my direction, he would have had trouble seeing me since I blended into the darkness around me.

I remained hidden, trying to figure out the man's function. It did not take long: he was the night guard, of course. Why hadn't I thought of it before? I sighed with relief. My troubles were at an end. I wouldn't have to call the police. I would tell the man what had happened; he would have no reason not to believe me. Anyway, he could easily check the library's records and see that I had been a member in good standing for many years.

Even so, I had to adjust my approach to the circumstances. The night guard certainly did not expect someone to jump out of the darkness at him. Who knew how he would react? He might even aim his gun at me, and that was all I needed. I coughed and walked towards him slowly. After several steps I said in a mild, well-intentioned voice, "Good evening."

I had assumed he would stand up, perhaps even jump up from his chair. I would stop in that case and let him walk towards me, giving him a chance to collect his wits. Any sudden movement, even just walking toward him, would be inadvisable, since it could be interpreted as a threat. But, contrary to my expectations, the guard just raised his eyes towards me and returned my greeting, not the least bit surprised, as though my sudden appearance was quite natural: "Good evening. May I help you?"

I walked up to the counter. The man had a nicely trimmed, thick black moustache, but his hair was already turning gray. The suit he wore seemed of high quality. The handkerchief peeping out from his breast pocket was the same shade as his tie. I am unfamiliar with the dress code for library night guards, but I certainly hadn't expected this! The manager of the library might as well have stood in front of me, wearing his best suit.

"You see," I began, "I'm a little late..."

"You're not late at all," said the man behind the counter, interrupting me. "We work at night. This is a night library."

I stared at him in bewilderment. "Night library? I didn't even know they existed."

"Yes, they do. And have for a very long time. Although very little is known about us. Were you interested in a book?"

"Yes, if possible. I really enjoy reading on the weekend. I was already afraid I would finish up empty handed this time. It's really nice that books are available at night, too."

"Of course they are. Although the selection is different than during the day. We only have books of life."

I thought I had misunderstood. "Excuse me?"

"Books of life. You haven't heard of them?"

I shook my head. "I'm afraid not."

"Too bad. I certainly recommend them. Quite interesting reading. Contrary to widespread belief, real lives are often considerably more exciting than those that are invented."

"Which real lives?"

"Everyone's."

"What do you mean—everyone's?"

"Literally. The lives of all the people who ever existed."

I silently studied the man on the other side of the counter for several moments. "There must be a lot of them."

"Yes, there are. One hundred nine billion, four hundred eighty-three million, two hundred fifty-six thousand, seven hundred and ten. As of the moment you entered the library."

I did not reply at once. I hoped that he interpreted my silence as an expression of amazement at the information he had just given me. What was going on here? Who was this man? He wasn't the night guard—that was quite certain. I also doubted his claim to be the night librarian. Whoever he was, I had to be careful. I was locked in a dark, deserted library with him. I had to avoid any conflicts, not deny anything, not contradict him, not enter into unnecessary discussion. Just wait for a chance to get out of there with the least difficulty. Suddenly, I wasn't interested in books anymore.

"You don't say!" I said finally, trying to appear properly amazed.

"Yes, but don't let this enormous number give you the wrong impression. Even though there are so many lives, each one of them is unique and unrepeatable. Precious. That is why they deserve to be recorded. Thus the books of life."

"So, more than one hundred billion of them. That is truly a gigantic library!" I figured a little flattery wouldn't hurt.

"Yes." A proud smile appeared on the stranger's face. "And constantly growing. A daily update is made of books on the people who are living now. And there are more than six billion of them! With new additions arriving all the time. Mankind is multiplying unchecked."

I nodded in admiration. "If I understand you correctly, the books of life are some kind of diary."

"You might call them that. But they are very objective diaries. That is their main attraction. Nothing is left out, nothing is hidden, nothing is shown in a different way. They are perfectly true. Which is only fitting. Like documentary films. You'll see for yourself when you read one of the books of life. Which one would you like?"

I thought it over. "I wouldn't know. It's not easy to decide when there are so many to choose from. Which would you recommend?"

"Almost everyone chooses the book about himself first. Which is a little strange since they have already read that book, in a way. But many still find it full of surprises and revelations. People are mostly inclined to forget things or suppress them."

"Do you mean to say there is a book about me, too?" My surprise was not exactly feigned.

"Of course. Why should you be an exception?"

I hesitated briefly. "All right. I'll take the book about myself."

"Fine," replied the man in the dark suit. "Wait here, please. I'll bring it to you at once."

He got up and headed for the back room, leaving the door ajar behind him. I stood in the small circle of light around the counter. I started to feel warm. I still had no idea what was going on, but asking for the book would let me end the whole thing calmly. I would take the book he offered, thank him, and leave. Everything would be much simpler once I left the library.

What the man brought me several minutes later was not exactly a book. It resembled a large binder. A thick sheaf of pages stuck out from between brown cardboard covers. Noticing my puzzled look, he hurried to explain. "This is the only way to add new pages during the update. The book will only be bound when there is nothing more to add." He smiled at me again. "Luckily, in your case that time has not yet arrived."

I returned the smile and took the binder. It was quite heavy. My name and date of birth had been printed in large, blue letters on the cover. The place for the other date was blank. I put the binder under my arm, reached into my jacket pocket, and took out my library card. "Is this valid for the night library, too," I said, handing it to him, "or does it require separate membership?"

"No need. We do not stick to formalities here. You are already a member by virtue of the fact that our stacks contain a book about you. In any case, we don't lend books, so there is no need to keep records."

"You don't lend them?" I asked, confused. "Does that mean I can't take this with me?"

"Unfortunately, that's impossible. It's the only copy we have. Something might happen to it outside the library, and that would be an irreparable loss. All traces of you would be lost, everything kept inside. It would be as though you'd never lived. We cannot take such a risk. But you can read it here at your leisure." He pointed to the tables on the right. "Make yourself comfortable and turn on the lamp. You can have as much time as you need."

I shouldn't have accepted it. I should have thanked him for the offer, told him it was late, I was tired, promised to return another time, and left at once. But I didn't. Vain curiosity won out. It isn't every day you get to read a book in which you are the main character. I wouldn't keep it for long, just leaf through it, I told myself. I sat down at the nearest table, pushed the button on the table lamp and placed the binder in front of me. The stranger at the counter bowed his head, engrossed in his own work.

If I hadn't been in a hurry, I would have started at the beginning, although I wouldn't have been able to testify to the accuracy of the account. Who still remembers their earliest days? I turned the binder face down and opened it from the back. I wanted to see how up-to-date it was. This all seemed like a lot of fun, of course, but a flicker of apprehension rose somewhere in the back of my mind. I felt like someone who doesn't believe in fortune telling, standing before a clairvoyant who is about to tell him his future.

The last page had been filled with tiny writing. A heading with today's date straddled the middle of the page. I started reading from that spot. Somewhere towards the bottom I reached into my coat pocket and took out my movie ticket. I compared the row and seat numbers with the ones cited in the book of life. A lump formed in my throat. The last sentence brought vividly to memory the clock in the library foyer whose hands showed three minutes after eight.

I glanced at the man sitting in the librarian's chair, his position unchanged, and then looked around uncomfortably. I suddenly got the impression of invisible eyes piercing the darkness, staring at me from all sides. This sensation made it hard to concentrate on my reading. But I had to continue despite an overpowering feeling that I would certainly not like what was to come next.

I began to turn the pages impatiently, leaving the end of the binder, heading towards the past. I searched for special dates in my life, dates when something had happened that no one else would know about except me. Or should know. Or had a right to know. And yet they still knew. Everything was written down there before me, all the dry facts, like a court indictment. Every secret that I had hidden not only from others, but often from myself. I felt hopelessly naked, like a hardened criminal whose crimes have suddenly been disclosed to the public.

I closed the binder. Beads of sweat streamed down my forehead, and not just because I was wearing a coat. I sat there a while longer, unmoving, my eyes blank. Then I turned off the lamp and went slowly up to the counter. I put my alleged book of life upon it. The stranger smiled at me again, but I remained serious and dejected.

"This isn't a night library, right?" I said in a hushed voice. "This isn't a book of life, either. It's my dossier. And you are some kind of secret police, spying service, or whatever you're called. I don't know much about such things. Congratulations. You've done a wonderful job. I had no idea that such surveillance was possible. Truly unbelievable. And terrifying. All right, now what? You know literally everything about me. There's nothing you can accuse me of, but you've collected more than enough to keep a hold over me. So you can blackmail me. That's what you're up to, right? The only thing I don't understand is why you had to invent that fantastic story about the billions of life stories since time immemorial, when you could have done perfectly well without it. Particularly since it's not the least bit convincing."

"Nothing has been invented, although I don't blame you for thinking so. Almost everyone who reads his own book of life reaches the same conclusion as you. It's quite understandable."

"But the story has its weak spots. You overlooked some details. How, for example, did you know which binder to bring? I didn't introduce myself beforehand."

"We knew. Everyone goes to the night library sooner or later. It was your turn today. We were waiting for you."

"Really? Are you waiting for someone else after me, perhaps? If you are, I've got bad news for you. The entrance is locked. No one else can come in. And what kind of a night library is it that's locked at night, huh?" I hoped I sounded caustic enough.

"You're mistaken," replied the man behind the counter softly. "It's open. You'll see for yourself when you go downstairs."

We looked at each other for several moments in silence. The smile lingered on the stranger's face.

"Do you mean to say," I said finally, "that I am free to go?"

"Certainly. How could you be stopped? Libraries are free to enter and exit as you like. That's how it's always been. Night libraries are no exception. Unless there's something else you would like to read, nothing prevents you from leaving."

I didn't think twice. "I don't think I care to read anything else. Thank you."

"You're welcome. We are pleased that you visited us. Good night, sir." He took the binder, stood up, nodded to me, then walked into the back room.

"Good night," I replied, when he was already on the other side of the door.

I stayed in front of the counter a little while longer. The silence began to thicken around me. I could feel the ghostly eyes from the darkness stabbing me in the back. The man did not return. I turned and headed down the long, dark carpet at a faster pace than I had intended. I stopped at the end of the room and turned around briefly. The lamp had been turned off.

Holding onto the rail, I descended to the ground floor. I grabbed the doorknob, but didn't twist it. For the third time, the outcome of this simple movement filled me with apprehension. The previous times had been easier. I would not have been in any serious trouble if the door hadn't opened. It would only have caused a minor inconvenience. I would have been without anything to read over the weekend, or I would have had to call the police to come and get me out.

Now, however, I didn't dare think about my fate if the door turned out to be locked. I would be trapped with no way out. But I couldn't hesitate forever. The doorknob slowly turned. When I pulled the door, it glided smoothly towards me and wrapped me in a whirlwind of large snowflakes. I quickly went out and took in a deep breath of cold winter air. The door closed automatically behind me.

I stood in front of the library, hands in my pockets, collar raised. I had no reason to stay there, but somehow I didn't want to leave. Before I finally left, I turned once more towards the entrance. Not much could be seen through the glass. Just beyond the door rose an opaque wall of darkness. The clock hung from its very edge; the rod that attached it to the ceiling could not be seen in the darkness, so it seemed to float. My gaze passed fleetingly over that round, white surface with its hands and numbers. At first, I didn't realize the problem.

The nature of my new disturbance only became clear after I had taken a few steps away from the library. I stopped in my tracks, then rushed back to the entrance. I pressed my face against the glass and sheltered my eyes with my hands. A shiver ran down my spine. I stood back from the door, took off my glasses and raised my left wrist. The conviction that I would see something different was fragile and unstable, but what else remained? The feeling disappeared instantly, as happens to futile hopes. Both clocks, the one inside and mine outside, showed the same time: three minutes after eight.

I shook my head in disbelief. This simply could not be. I had spent at least an hour in the library. Maybe even an hour and a half. That was quite certain. Every moment was still vivid to me. My experiences could not have been imaginary or an illusion. On the other hand, time cannot stand still. Regardless of their power, the secret police still cannot stop time. So what had happened? There had to be an explanation.

There was only one way to find the answer: by entering the library a second time. The thought did not appeal to me at all, but reliving an impossible mystery for the rest of my life would have been even harder. A shiver went through me when I reached for the doorknob. I pushed the door but it didn't move. I tried once again, harder, but it didn't budge. The library was locked, just as it should have been. Libraries don't stay open at night. There are no night libraries. Working hours were over and the personnel had gone home. I was too late.

I had to resign myself to the situation, particularly since I didn't know what to do. I couldn't break into the library, of course. Even if I'd wanted to, how could I have done it? I was no burglar, I hadn't the talent for it. I hushed the voices inside me that opposed my withdrawal. What else could I do? What was the point of standing there in the darkness and the snow? I would only catch cold needlessly or appear suspicious to some cop on his beat. I put my hands back into my pockets, hunched my shoulders, and headed down the street through the thick swarm of snowflakes.

I didn't get very far this time, either. I stopped in mid-step, next to the nearest lamppost, although I couldn't figure out why at first. The vague feeling came over me that I had missed something. I had overlooked some detail. I racked my brain, but it was just out of reach, like a word on the tip of your tongue that you can't remember. I looked toward the sky. The wide, orange beam of light from the street lamp was dotted with innumerable flakes, slowly floating downwards, carried by the wind. The moment they started to fall on my face, it dawned on me.

I turned and hurried back to the library entrance, almost slipping in the slush. I no longer needed to shield my eyes from the outside light. I no longer truly needed even to look inside because, even before I did, I knew what I would see, in spite of the darkness within the library. The handle of my umbrella was sticking out of the cylindrical brass stand.

4. Infernal Library

The guard escorting me stopped before a door
in the hallway and knocked. He waited for a few
moments and then seemed to hear permission
to enter, although nothing reached my ears. He
opened the door, pushed me forward without a
word, and stepped inside after me, grabbing hold
of my shoulder to keep me there as he closed the
door behind him. His grasp was unnecessarily
firm since I had already stopped, not knowing
what else to do. He probably didn't know how to
be more gentle. We stood by the door, obviously
awaiting new orders.

As with everything else I had seen so far, the
ceiling was extremely high. This impression was
accentuated here because the distance to the ceiling was considerably greater than the length and
width of the room. I was suddenly overcome by
the dizzying feeling that it would be more natural

for the floor and one of the side walls to change places. But, of course, I could not expect the natural order of things to be maintained in this place. That time had passed for good. Who knew what unusual experiences were in store for me. I had to prepare myself for much worse.

The room was poorly lit and sparsely furnished. Hanging from the ceiling on a long wire, a weak bulb covered by a round metal shade shed most of its light on a backless wooden chair that stood by itself in the middle of the room. A man sat at a desk opposite the door, his back to the wall. Only visible above the shoulders, he concentrated on the computer screen in front of him. By the indistinct glow of the monitor, which created no shadow, his long face seemed almost ghostly pale. His short, thick beard appeared grizzled in the odd light and he wore semicircular reading glasses. I could not determine his age. He might have been anywhere from his early forties to his late fifties.

He didn't seem to notice us. The guard and I stood patiently by the door, as motionless as statues. Finally, without taking his eyes off the screen, the man raised his left hand and made a brief, vague gesture, which nonetheless had a clear meaning for the guard. He grabbed my shoulder roughly once again and led me towards the chair under the light. He released me only when I had sat down, then stood directly behind me.

The Library

While I waited, my gaze began to wander. The feeling of confinement caused by the height of the room was intensified by the uniformity of color around me. A sickly shade of olive-gray covered everything: the walls, the ceiling, the floor, the chair, the table. Even the monitor was olive-gray. The paint on the walls was cracked and peeling in places, showing patches of dry plaster the color of a stormy sky. It felt as if we were inside a faded and worn shoebox, once green, placed on end.

The room might have been less gloomy if there had been a window, even one with bars. But there were no windows. Working in a place like this could only be considered punishment. I looked at the person behind the monitor with a mixture of pity and dread. Even if I disregarded all the rest, there was certainly no reason to expect good of someone forced to work here for any period of time.

The deep silence in the room was suddenly broken by fingers tapping on a keyboard that I couldn't see. The rapid typing did not last long. When he was finished, the man raised his head, took off his glasses and laid them on the desk next to him. Then he squinted and pinched the bridge of his nose with his thumb and forefinger. He remained in this position for several moments before opening his eyes and nodding to the guard. The guard moved off at a brisk pace. The metal door opened with a squeak and then closed behind him.

We looked at each other without speaking for some time. I felt uncomfortable under his silent inspection, which expressed more aversion and bad temper than harshness or threat. I quickly realized that he wasn't the least bit happy about the upcoming conversation with me. He behaved like someone who has been doing the same job for too long to be able to find anything appealing in it. I had seen that expression on the faces of some older investigators and judges. Finally the man sighed, drew his fingers across his high forehead and broke the silence.

"You realize where you are, don't you?" He had a deep, drawling voice.

"In hell," I replied after hesitating a moment.

"That's right. Although we don't use that name anymore. Are you aware of why you have come to this place?"

I didn't answer right away. It was clear to me that there was no sense in hiding or denying anything, but I didn't exactly have to incriminate myself, either. "I can guess..."

"You can guess?" He raised his voice. "Even here we rarely see a dossier like this." He knocked the crook of his middle finger against the screen.

"I might be able to explain..."

"Don't!" he said, cutting me off. "Spare me, if you please! How inconsiderate you are, all of you who sit there. It isn't enough that I have to learn about the disgusting things you've done; you want me to listen to your phony, slime-ball explanations, too. They make me even sicker than the crimes themselves. In any case, there's nothing to explain. Everything is perfectly clear. We know all about you. Every detail. Would you be here if that weren't the case?"

"Mistakes do happen..." I noted softly.

"There are no mistakes," replied the man. "And even if there were, it's too late to rectify them. There's no way out of here. Once you're in, you stay for good."

I knew that, of course. Everyone knows that. But I still had to try.

"What about repentance? Does that mean anything?" I asked in the humblest of voices.

This time he didn't have to say anything. His expression told me exactly what he thought about my remorse.

"Don't waste your breath. I have no time for such nonsense. I'm inundated with work. The world has never been like this before. Can you imagine the burden on my shoulders?"

I could imagine, but since the question was rhetorical, I just shrugged. For a moment I thought

59

the man wanted to complain to me about his hardships, but then he changed his mind.

"Forget it. It's not important. Let's get to the point. We have to find out what would suit you best."

"As punishment?" I asked cautiously.

"We call it therapy."

"Burning in fire is therapy?"

"Who's talking about burning in fire?"

"Maybe being boiled in oil or drawn and quartered..."

"Don't be vulgar! This isn't the Middle Ages!"

"Sorry, I didn't know..."

"It's simply unbelievable how many people come here with preconceived notions. Do you think we live outside the times? That nothing changes here? Would this go along with such barbaric brutality?" He tapped the side of the monitor.

"Of course not," I readily agreed.

"Every age has its own hell. Today it's a library."

I blinked in bewilderment. "A library?"

"Yes. A place where books are read. You have heard about libraries? Why is everyone so amazed when they find out?"

"It's a bit...unexpected."

"Only if you give it perfunctory consideration. Once you delve into the matter, you see that there's nothing unusual about it."

"It never would have crossed my mind."

"To tell you the truth, we were also a bit surprised at first. But what the computer told us was unequivocal. It is quite a useful machine."

He paused. Several moments passed before I understood what was expected of me. "Quite useful, indeed," I repeated.

"Particularly for statistical research. When we input data about everyone here, the trait that linked by far the greatest number of our inmates, 84.12 percent to be precise, was their aversion to reading. This was understandable for 26.38 percent, since they are completely illiterate. But what about the 47.71 percent who, although literate, had never picked up a single book, as though fearing the plague? The remaining ten or so percent read something here and there, but they'd wasted their time since it was totally worthless."

I nodded. "Who would have thought?"

He looked at me askance. "Why does that seem strange to you? Take yourself. How many books have you read?"

I thought it over briefly, trying to remember. "Well, er, not a whole lot, to tell the truth."

"Not a whole lot? I'll tell you exactly how many." The rapid sound of typing on the keyboard was heard once more. "In the past twenty-eight years of your life you started two books. You got halfway through the fourth page of the first, and in the second you didn't get beyond the introductory paragraph."

"It didn't catch my interest," I replied contritely.

"Really? And other things did?"

"I never suspected that not reading was a mortal sin."

"It isn't. Although the world would be a much better place if it were. No one's ever been sent to hell because they didn't read. That's why this trait was overlooked until we brought in the computer. But when, thanks to the computer, we noticed this connection, we were able to take advantage of it. In several ways. You might even say that it led to a true reform of hell."

"No one knows anything about that."

"Of course no one knows. How could anyone know? That's where all those prejudices come from. This place has never been the way most people imagine it: an eternal torture chamber run by merciless sadists. Tell me, do you smell that sulfur everyone talks about so much?"

I sniffed the air around me. It was dry and stale, a little musty. "No," I had to admit.

"We were simply a jail. With a few special features, that's true, but the system here differed very little from what you found in your jails. We treated our inmates here the same way you treated yours. Why should we be any different? If there was brutality and abuse here, that meant we were following your example. As conditions improved over time in your jails, the situation here became more bearable. Things went so far there was a danger of going against the basic idea of hell."

"What do you mean?"

"Recently your jails have almost been turned into recreation centers. You might even say they're modest hotels. You're the best judge of that; you spent a lot of time in jail, and it wasn't the least uncomfortable, right?"

I thought it over. "No, you're right, although the food wasn't always that good everywhere. Especially dessert."

A fleeting sigh escaped from the man behind the monitor. "There, you see. Well, now, we couldn't allow some of those privileges here. Weekend leaves, for instance. Or using cellular phones. How would that look?"

"But that would make it much easier to serve your time..."

"Perhaps. But it must never be forgotten that this is hell, after all. So we found ourselves in a bind. We couldn't follow the liberalization of conditions in your jails any longer. We were threatened with the one thing we have been accused of since time immemorial: being the incarnation of inhumanity and jeopardizing human rights. Luckily, that's when we found out about people not reading."

"Excuse me, but I don't see the connection."

"It was a simple matter. We made reading compulsory for everyone. This enabled us to combine the beautiful with the useful. First of all, our inmates could get rid of the main shortcoming that brought them here. If they had read more, they would have had less time and motive for misdeeds. Reading for them is truly healing. That is why we consider it therapy, not punishment, even though it might be a little late. But it is never really too late for something like that. And what do we call the place where everyone loves to read?"

"A library?"

The man spread his arms. "Of course. And a library is the last place to be accused of violating human rights, wouldn't you say? At the same time, this step removed the extremely embarrassing tarnish we had acquired. Furthermore, we turned out to be considerably more humane than your jails. They have libraries, of course, but what's the point, since they are almost never used? It's as though they don't even exist. Take your own case once again. Did you ever go into a library in one of the many jails you were in?"

"I didn't even know they had them," I replied truthfully.

"What did I tell you? But don't worry, you'll soon have a chance to make up for what you've missed. And much more than that, in effect. Before you is literally a whole eternity of reading."

I stared at the man for several moments without speaking. "So that's my punishment? Reading?"

"Therapy."

"Therapy, yes. There won't be anything else?" I tried to suppress the sound of relief in my voice, but without success.

"Nothing else, of course. You will sit in your cell and read. That's all. You won't have any other obligation. I must, however, draw your attention to the fact that eternity is a very long time. You might get bored with reading at some point. That happens to many of our inmates and then they become very clever. My, what tricks they resort to, giving the impression that they're reading, even though they aren't. But we have ways to see through all those crafty ploys. In such cases we must, unfortunately, use forceful means to get them to return to reading. With the most resistant and stubborn they are sometimes rather painful, I'm afraid."

"What about human rights? Humanity?"

"We don't lay a hand on them. This is exclusively for their own good. We can't let them harm themselves out of spiritual indolence, can we?"

"I suppose not," I replied, not quite convinced.

"Those are the main things you should know. You will grow accustomed to conditions here. It will probably be a little difficult at first, until you get used to it, but you will finally realize that reading offers incomparable satisfaction. Everyone becomes aware of this during eternity, some sooner and some later. I hope in the meantime that you behave in a mature and sober manner and do not compel us to resort to force. That will make it nice and easy for everyone."

Since my unquestioning agreement was clearly understood, I nodded. For the first time, the corners of the man's mouth turned up a little, forming the shadow of a smile.

"Fine. Now let's see which therapy would suit you best. What kind of reading material would you prefer?"

It was a difficult question, so I took my time answering it. "Maybe detective stories," I said finally, in a half-questioning tone.

"Ah, certainly not!" replied the man, frowning again. "That would be like giving a sick man poison instead of medicine. No, you need something quite the opposite. Something mild, gentle, enriching. Pastoral works, for example. Yes, that is the right choice for your soul. Idylls. We often prescribe them. They have a truly wondrous effect."

He saw an expression on my face that might have been disgust. When he spoke again his voice had returned to its initial sharpness.

"If you think this unjust, you can take consolation in the fact that I would give anything to be in your shoes. Enjoying idylls. At least for a while. But I can't, unfortunately. They won't let me. Instead, I am forced to read exclusively the abominations and baseness that simply gush out of here. Like water from a broken dam." He tapped the monitor again, this time on top. "And eternity for me is no shorter than it is for you. That's not fair. Whenever you hit crisis-point, just think how much I envy you, and you'll feel better."

He stopped talking. The incongruous height and dreary color of the room suddenly seemed to collapse in on him, twisting his face into a mask of contempt and despair. He looked at me a moment longer, his eyes turning blank. Before he reached for his glasses and put them on again, he turned his head towards the door behind me. He didn't say a word, but it squeaked right away. The guard's firm hand found my shoulder. I got up off

the chair under the light bulb and headed outside. On the way, I took another look at the man
behind the desk. He had almost completely sunk
behind the monitor, engrossed in a new dossier. A
moment later the door hid him from my view, and
I set off down the hall with the guard towards my
cell, where an eternity of reading awaited me as
well.

5. Smallest Library

I didn't realize I had one book too many until I got home. I should have had three in the plastic bag, but I took out four volumes. The old man had put the books into an old, crumpled bag, stained with something black on the outside. I had made no remark about the bag, not wanting to offend him. How could I tell him that it made no difference to me if the books he gave me got wet in the rain? Everything would have been different, of course, had I brought an umbrella, but it hadn't looked like rain when I'd left home.

The old man perfectly matched the bag he had given me. Greatly advanced in age, he had a wrinkled face and gray beard in which the rare streaks of dark hair resembled bits of leftover food. His clothes were no different from his face. His long, threadbare and dirty coat, which almost touched the ground, was patched here and there and, although the weather did not call for it, buttoned all the way to the top. It was early spring, but unusually warm and filled with sudden showers. Had I met this man anywhere else, I might easily think he was a beggar.

The old man's unsavory appearance, however, did not stand out among the used book sellers who displayed their wares all year long, even during the cold winter months, every Saturday at the same place, under the Great Bridge. They would bring folding tables, plastic crates for mineral water, or even large cardboard boxes that they would cover with newspapers, thus creating a makeshift stand. If it weren't for the books on these stands, the spot would resemble a flea market.

But looks can deceive. These were by no means simple peddlers with only the most basic information about their goods. Although one would never guess it from their unkempt, almost tramp-like appearance and the location of their stalls, a few words with them would quickly reveal that they were excellent book connoisseurs. Should you express an interest in one of the books on display, the seller would provide you with a mass of information about the author, publisher, reviews, reader reception, possible previous or later editions. Sometimes you might even hear a detailed history of a specific copy that was more exciting than all the rest.

The Library

The information was as trustworthy as if you had opened a literary encyclopaedia. Nothing was hidden or embellished, as might be expected of those who are only interested in selling their goods. Sometimes you would have the strange impression that what you were being told was intended to dissuade you from actually buying the book.

For more than a year I had been walking under the Great Bridge every Saturday, above all for these conversations with the booksellers. In the end I would buy one book or another, not because I wanted to have it so much as to compensate these people whose words provided the impetus for what I myself had been trying to write.

Over time, I became better acquainted with some of the booksellers I habitually saw there, and so enjoyed their additional esteem as a regular customer. Whenever I appeared, they would pull books out from under the counter that they'd kept for me, and the conversations we struck up would not be interrupted, I believe, even at the cost of losing another customer who might be ready to spend quite a bit of money. Several times I was tempted to propose that we continue our discussions elsewhere, but I held back. For some reason, I had the feeling that it would not be the same. Indeed, it was as if they could not exist anywhere else but here.

I had never met the old man before. Since all the places under the bridge were occupied, he had set up shop at the very end, where there was no longer any protection from above, as though he had been excommunicated by the others. He could only stay there until the first drops of rain forced him to seek cover. This would not have been difficult since he was the only one with a mobile stand. It was a cart that had once, long ago, been used to sell ice cream: a wooden box with two large wheels and two long handles for pushing it. I hadn't seen one since childhood. The bright paint that had once decorated this affair was completely faded or peeled, but I could still make out the shape of an ice cream cone with three large scoops painted on the front.

The other sellers would let me look at the books without offering their comments. They would only strike up a conversation with me when I asked a question or had selected a book. That was the generally accepted custom. The old man either did not know this or did not care. He addressed me as soon as I walked up to his stand.

"I have what you're looking for," he said in the hoarse voice typical of chain smokers.

"How do you know I'm even looking for something?" I replied a little abrasively, glancing over the old books that covered the top of the cart. The two conical metal lids that had covered the two openings for ice cream had been replaced by an unfinished bare board. A pile of old books, seemingly dumped out of a bag, lay on top of the board.

"It's not hard to tell. It shows on your face."

"Shows on my face?" I repeated, bewildered, examining the old man. That very instant I realized what I had missed when I first glanced at his face. His head was turned towards me but not his eyes. The eyes stared to the side, unfocussed, blurred. The man was blind.

"Yes," he said. "If you know how to look."

"So that's it," I said, nodding. The awkward feeling that came over me only intensified when I realized the senselessness of this movement.

The old man was suddenly seized by a fit of coughing, hollow and hoarse, like the echo of distant thunder. It seemed to come from the very depths of his lungs. He put one bony hand over his mouth, the other on his chest, and bowed his head. He stayed in that position for a while.

"You are a writer, aren't you?" he said in a whisper, after catching his breath.

"Does that show on my face, too?" I asked, also in a low voice.

He didn't reply at once, wheezing for a bit. "No, but there's a smell about you. Writers have a smell. The harder the time they're having, the stronger the smell. You didn't know that?"

Zoran Živković

Inadvertently I sniffed the air around me. The prevailing smell came from the river: humid, sour, with traces of rotting debris brought by the spring floods. "No, I didn't," I had to admit.

"It makes no difference. What's important is that there is a remedy. We'll find it right away." He started to examine the pile in front of him with his fingers. He took book after book, felt it lightly, and then put it back with the others or set it aside, as though able to see with his hands. Finally, when he had made his choice, he held out three books. "Here, this is what you need. They will help you."

I hesitated briefly, then accepted the offered volumes. They were bedraggled-looking. One had no cover at all, its front and back pages dog-eared. Another had been destroyed by someone's merciless scribbling. And the binding of the third was so broken it was in tatters. In addition, dust had accumulated in all three books. I had no reason to buy them, especially since I already had them in much better condition.

Nonetheless, I decided to take them. They would be of no use to me, but how could I refuse a blind old man? However, it wasn't just compassion. His cleverness deserved some reward. The bit about writers having a smell was pretty good. I might be able to use it somewhere. Although, of course, he had not recognized me by any smell.

The Library

As I was rushing home, I realized that there was only one way he could have known my profession. Several stands before his cart I had spoken briefly with one of the sellers of whom I was a regular customer. He asked how my new book was coming, and I had given a vague answer. The man could see that I didn't feel like talking about it and had changed the subject. We hadn't been that close to the old man and we were surrounded by a noisy crowd, so that under normal circumstances he would not have heard us. But people who have lost their sight have extremely sharp hearing.

"How much do I owe you?" I asked, reaching for my wallet.

The old man coughed again. This time the hacking lasted a bit longer. "You owe me a lot," he said at last. "But not for the books. They are free."

I looked in bewilderment at his empty eyes. "Why would you give them away?"

"Because that is the only way for you to get them. I don't sell books."

I expected him to say something else, but he clearly felt that this answer was sufficient.

"You have put me in an awkward position," I said after a short pause. "I don't know how to repay you."

"Forget it. Give me the books so I can put them in a bag for you. It will rain soon and they might get wet, and that would be a real shame."

I looked towards the bit of sky not blocked by the bridge. Clouds had started to gather, but there were still patches of clear sky, so it didn't look like it was about to rain. I didn't say anything, however, since the old man appeared quite sure of himself. Maybe blind people can forecast the weather in addition to hearing quite well.

I put the three books into his outstretched hand and he bent down behind the cart, opening the door down there. He felt around inside and finally took out a crumpled, stained bag with the three books inside it. At least that's what I thought at the time. It was only upon returning home that I discovered that he had added a fourth. He must have done it then. There had been no other opportunity.

"Thank you very much," I said, taking the bag gingerly with two fingers. I was glad the man couldn't see my expression. "Goodbye. I hope we'll see each other again soon." As soon as I'd said it, I realized how inappropriate this greeting was, but it was too late to retract it.

"Farewell," replied the old man, politely overlooking my blunder.

On the way home, I thought it might be best if I got rid of the unwanted gift en route. But the sky dissuaded me from my intention. When I climbed up onto the Great Bridge, I saw that the old man had been right. Storm clouds were rushing in from the west, dragging a dense curtain of rain with them. I had to hurry if I didn't want to get caught in a downpour. I had no time now to look for a trashcan in which to dump the bag. Just as I stepped inside my front door, rain began to fall.

I could have put the bag in the garbage can in the kitchen, but I didn't. What I had been prepared to do outside without hesitation suddenly seemed inappropriate indoors. Sacrilegious, in fact. One doesn't throw books away, after all. Not even such worthless copies. I would put them out of sight somewhere. That would be the same as if I had thrown them away, but my conscience would be clear.

The fourth book that appeared when I emptied the bag stood out from the others. First of all, it was in excellent condition, although also an old edition. I turned it over in my hands, staring with bewildered curiosity. It took some time for me to realize there wasn't even a speck of dust on my fingers.

Nothing had been written on the chestnut-colored canvas cover, but that was not unusual. The book had probably had a paper cover that had been lost in the meantime. In the middle of the front cover was a shallow imprint, the stylized depiction of a pointed quill, an inkpot and an image resembling a sheet of parchment. The pages were edged in a shade of brown that matched the cover.

I opened the book. After a chestnut-colored blank flyleaf, the words *The Smallest Library* were written at the top of the first page in tiny, slanted letters. This didn't exactly fit the appearance and format of the volume. Someone had been too modest when naming the edition. Something more imposing would have been preferable.

I turned the page and the first surprise awaited me. The second page where information about the book should have been given was blank, while the third page contained only one word, which I assumed must have been the title of the work. But the author's name was missing. Filled with doubt, I looked for several moments at the inordinate whiteness before me. This was unusual to say the least.

Then I realized where I might find the copyright information. Some publishers put that page in the back. Although this would not explain the author's missing name, it was still worthwhile to check. I leafed through the book quickly, noting as I did so that it was a novel whose chapters had only numbers and not titles. When I reached the end, I discovered there was no information there, either. After the last printed page there was just one white one, then the chestnut-colored back flyleaf, and finally the cover.

The Library

I had therefore received from the old man an anonymous edition by an anonymous writer. I had yet to hear of such a combination, but it clearly did not follow that this was impossible. Although I am not uninformed about the world of books, my knowledge is by no means comprehensive. There was one place, however, where all information about absolutely all officially published works should be found: the National Library. I closed the book, laid it on my desk, and switched on the computer.

The National Library web site made it possible to execute rapid searches, even though it had an enormous stock of books. I typed the only information I had into the space marked "title." I was convinced that this would solve the mystery because any other outcome would be quite unimaginable. That would mean this was an unregistered edition, shedding new light on the whole matter. The old man's appearance may not have been exemplary, but I doubted he was ready to get involved in any nefarious dealings with books. In any case, the other booksellers under the Great Bridge, proud of their honesty, would not allow him to do that.

Nonetheless, about half a minute later the message on the screen told me that a work under that title did not exist in the catalogue of the National Library. I sighed deeply and drew my left hand through my hair. This was becoming awkward.

Perhaps I had been wrong about the old man after all. I thought back to parts of our brief conversation that I'd skipped over lightly, although they should have aroused my suspicions.

Still, it was hard for me to believe that the blind man with the ice cream cart had been dishonest. My intuition, which rarely erred, protected him. Without taking my eyes off the screen where the message about the unsuccessful search quivered dully, I tried to find some way around the seemingly inexorable conclusion that something illegal was going on. The only extenuating circumstance I could think of was that the book had been a present and had not been sold, which excluded any self-interest. This, however, could not be used as an excuse for the fact that the title did not exist in the National Library catalogue.

Then, like a drowning man grasping at straws, I thought of something highly unlikely. Perhaps I had remembered the title incorrectly. I was certain I hadn't, for I'd just closed the book and the word had been simple and short, but sometimes such commonplace oversights can occur. Maybe only one letter had been different. After all, computers are very literal machines. I picked up the brown book from the desk in front of me and opened it again.

What I saw on the third page simply could not have been true. A lump formed in my throat. The difference was much more than one letter. A completely different title, consisting not of one word but three, greeted me. The book started to tremble and I stared at it in disbelief for several long moments, until I finally realized my hands were shaking. I had to place them in my lap to calm them. I squinted at the new writing, doing my utmost to find some explanation for this impossibility, but I couldn't think of anything. A book cannot change its title by itself. Everyone knows that. But it had just happened. What kind of trick present had the old man slipped me? And why?

I could not find the answer to this question just sitting there helplessly, staring at the third page. I had to do something. But what? Take a closer look at the book, perhaps? The first time I had just flipped through it. If there was some trick involved, that would be the best way to find out. But the chestnut-colored volume lay motionless in my suddenly sweaty hands a little while. It required considerable willpower to raise it again.

I turned another page—and stared wide-eyed at the beginning of the text on the fifth page. It was a novel, as I had expected, but no longer the one from a moment before. This time the chapter was denoted by a title rather than a number. And the letters were a different size: smaller, with less space between the lines. I was holding a completely new book.

This was too much. I reacted as though someone had tossed me a burning object: I threw it away from me and jumped off my desk chair. The book fell on the keyboard and pressed some keys. The National Library site suddenly disappeared from the screen and the speakers emitted a high, broken squeak.

If not for the noise I wouldn't have dared touch the book again. But I couldn't stand the sound; it grated against my overwrought nerves. Carefully, as though picking up something that might bite me, I took the book off the keyboard. The squeaking stopped at once, but the screen still had no picture.

I stood in the middle of my study beside the chair, now at some distance from the desk, and held the book out in front of me. I had the feeling something was about to happen, but I couldn't guess what, so I didn't know how to prepare myself. Several slow, tense minutes passed. When nothing happened, I realized it was foolish to stand there, waiting. I had to act.

Having returned somewhat to my senses, I concluded I had only two choices. I could put the book back in the dirty bag, add the three others, and throw them all away at once, not in the kitchen garbage can, but in a dumpster outside, as far away as possible, maybe even in the river, in spite of the rain that still poured down. I would thus be free of the cause of my troubles.

Or, I could open the book again. That didn't appeal to me at all. I shrank from what I might find there. Once I had been through an earthquake. The most unpleasant part of that experience had been losing the solid ground under my feet, something I had always counted on to be there. Here I risked shaking an even more important foothold: reality.

But it was too late. Reality had already been shaken to its foundations. I could remove the book physically, but not from my memory. I could not continue to live a tranquil life, pretending nothing had happened. That would be like burying my head in the sand. Sooner or later, I would start to buckle under the weight of unanswered questions. So I actually had no choice.

I opened the canvas cover slowly, as though something might jump out of the book. Somehow I already knew what I would see on the third page, but I still started a little when I saw the new title. This time it consisted of two words. I didn't have to leaf through the book to be convinced it was a new novel.

But I did so anyway in order to check something else that had occurred to me. Turning several pages at a time, I soon reached the end. The typeface was now large, double spaced, and the chapters had both a number and a title. I went back to the beginning in the same way. There was no change. It seemed that the change only happened when I closed the book. The work stayed the same as long as the book was kept open.

I closed the book, then opened it again. That was it! By some magic, I had a new novel. I repeated this simple operation and smiled with pleasure at the same outcome. I had not come a single step closer to solving the problem, but at least I knew what was in store for me, so the tension eased a bit. It's amazing how much easier it is to accept the impossible once you are no longer afraid of it.

To show myself I no longer feared the chestnut-colored book, I started to open and close it quickly. I watched in fascination as the titles on the third page changed each time. I was filled with something like the ingenuous excitement that overcomes a child who has been given an amusing toy that produces unusual effects. I thought for a moment that the title of the edition was quite fitting after all. This was truly the smallest library, but by number of volumes, not titles. Indeed, what can be smaller than one single volume?

Then, after I had opened and closed the book a dozen times, I suddenly froze in mid-motion. The question that dawned on me suddenly turned my delight into something close to horror. What happened to the work after I closed the book? My discoveries so far indicated that it disappeared without a trace. Each title appeared only once. That meant that I had just lost more than ten books irretrievably with my thoughtlessness!

The Library

I couldn't let this happen again. I held the book open firmly with both hands, so it wouldn't close by accident. I started to think feverishly what to do. How could I save something as short-lived as a work that only existed so long as the book was open? Nothing came to mind. I have never been good at coping under pressure. That's why I can never write to deadlines. Then, when I was ready to sink into despair, something so obvious occurred to me that I would surely have slapped myself on the forehead if my hands had been free. Photocopying, of course!

There was no need to hurry. I could wait for the rain to stop. Spring showers don't last long, and the work now between the covers was safe as long as I kept the book open. However, my patience ran out. I held the book in one hand, fully open though that wasn't necessary, and rushed to the vestibule. I grabbed my coat and umbrella and quickly went out into the hall. Since my hands were full, I had a bit of trouble putting on my coat. Once I got outside, I had to lower the umbrella all the way to my head, the brown volume under my chin, in order to protect it from the heavy downpour.

I splashed along the wet pavement quickly, taking no notice of the fact that my shoes were full of water after only a few steps and my pant legs were soaked almost to the knee. Luckily, the small stationery store that had a photocopier was not far.

When I entered the store, shaking my umbrella after me, the owner looked at me in amazement. The woman clearly had not expected any customers in such a cloudburst. She must have wondered what urgent matter had forced me to come in just then, but she didn't say anything.

I said that I needed to photocopy something and waved the open book. I didn't give any explanation, although it would have been proper to do so. What, in any case, could I have said? She kindly offered to do it herself, but I declined the offer. I did so unnecessarily roughly because I was terrified at the possibility of someone else getting hold of the volume. The woman shrugged her shoulders and indicated the machine in the corner, then went back to her reading behind the counter.

I placed the book on the glass, lowered the heavy plastic cover and pressed the green button. The bright light went back and forth and a moment later a copy of the third page emerged from the side opening. At least that's what I hoped would happen. But there was nothing there. I turned the paper over, thinking the print was on the other side. Both sides were blank. I raised the lid and turned over the book. The title was still there, but it was invisible to the machine.

Noticing that I was turning over the book and the piece of paper, the storekeeper asked me if anything was wrong. Did I need help? I quickly replied no, everything was fine. In order to allay her doubts, I continued with the photocopying. I turned new pages, pressed the button on top, and completely empty pages continued to come out of the machine. From where the woman was standing, she couldn't see them, and she soon lowered her eyes to the newspaper in front of her, convinced that her strange customer had found his way.

The senseless photocopying was not so useless after all. It gave me a chance to steady my nerves after this new surprise. So I couldn't photocopy the book. I assumed that the same thing would happen if I photographed or scanned it. I shouldn't waste time on that. What was I going to do about the potentially short life of the individual works? I could not keep the book open all the time to save one book, because then all the others would become inaccessible. And if I wanted access to another work, this one would disappear forever. I couldn't see a way out of this conundrum.

Then a dark thought formed in my head, sending a shiver through me. Maybe that was the whole point. Maybe the whole thing was devised intentionally to be a Catch-22 situation. A very spiteful and malicious person stood behind *The Smallest Library*. Someone brazenly pretending to be a blind, benevolent old man with an ice cream cart, who generously handed out books. If I wanted to escape this trap, I would have to face him again.

I picked up the fifty-some empty pages, folded them lengthwise and put them under my arm. I hesitated briefly after raising the plastic lid, then quickly closed the book and put it in the large pocket of my raincoat. One title more or less—what was the difference? Approaching the counter, I put down a bill that was more than enough to cover what I owed her. I left without a word, feeling her inquisitive eyes on my back.

It was still raining, but now only small drops came sprinkling down. I opened my umbrella and headed briskly towards the Great Bridge, taking a shortcut. In an alley, I threw the bundle of blank papers into the first container without stopping. As I loped forward, the clouds first became lighter, then thinned out and finally, when I was already close to my destination, rays from the hidden sun poked through them here and there.

There were still a lot of people under the bridge. Many who didn't have an umbrella, as I hadn't at first, stood on the edge of the covered part waiting for the rain to stop so they could leave. They blocked my view of the far end, where the old man had set up his cart. But as I made my way to the middle, where the crowd thinned out, I realized I wouldn't find him there. He had been under the open sky before, so the downpour had certainly caused him to find shelter somewhere under the wide metal structure.

I started to turn around, searching, but there was no trace of the old ice cream cart. I certainly would not fail to see it. The space under the bridge was rather large, but it would be impossible to pass unnoticed there. Had the old man left during my absence? That seemed unlikely. Would a blind man pushing a bulky cart go out in such a thunderstorm? No, that would be reckless and dangerous. Unless, of course, the blindness and the rest had been a sham.

I wandered through the stands a while longer, not knowing what else to do, as my frustration mounted. Of the many questions besieging me, one slowly started to outweigh the others. Why me? Why had this happened to me, of all people? What set me apart from the others gathered in this place? The fact that I am a writer? A writer who hasn't been able to write anything worthwhile for quite some time? Wasn't that damnation enough? Why did I have to be given this book?

As I walked aimlessly, I found myself close to the seller I had talked to just before the fateful meeting. I thought for a moment to ask him about the old man. He could hardly have escaped his notice. But I didn't do so. Asking questions would only get me entangled in a web of explanations about something that had completely escaped my understanding. I might even be forced to take the volume out of my pocket and show it to him, which I wanted to avoid at all costs. But one other thing also discouraged me from conversation, something I dreaded most of all. What if the seller said he hadn't seen a blind man with an ice cream cart?

There was no reason to stay here any longer. The weather had cleared up considerably. Now there were far fewer visitors under the Great Bridge. This time I headed home slowly, no longer in a hurry. I hadn't gone very far when I became aware of the smells. First of ozone, then many others in dense clusters everywhere, brought out by the rain: the smell of new leaves in the tops of the linden trees, the damp young grass, the covering of humus in the little park, the washed flowers in the flowerpots. It seemed that even the water covering the sidewalk and pavement in large puddles had a smell of its own.

And at intervals, somewhere in the background of these strong smells, dampened by them, I detected a weaker smell that seemed vaguely familiar. It was omnipresent or else was following me. It was unpleasant, like the stink of sweat, but different, arousing thoughts of something strenuous and hard. Even painful. I tried to decipher it, but without success. The effort was not in vain, however. Quite unexpectedly, as I tried to figure out the mysterious smell, I thought of something which should have occurred to me a lot sooner.

The Library

Before the photocopying, certainly. I quickened my pace almost to a run.

I took the monitor and keyboard off my desk since I didn't need them. I could have done the job faster by computer, but I never wrote using the computer. Instead, I took out a large notebook that had been empty for a long time. I didn't start to copy right away, however. When I picked up my pen, I was filled with the fear that this might lead nowhere. What if the pen left no mark, even though brand-new? I didn't know. Yet what could I lose by trying? Things certainly couldn't be worse than they already were.

I was unable to suppress a sigh of relief when the title of the novel appeared several moments later at the top of the first page. Clear and legible. I closed my notebook briefly and opened it again. No miracle took place. The writing was still there, as it ought to be. I turned the page in the book and sat back comfortably in my chair. Under the title I wrote "First Chapter" and then continued to the first paragraph.

Long and difficult work lay ahead of me. The novel was printed in tiny, single-spaced letters. But hardship is to be expected in the profession of writer. There is no respite. There are no shortcuts. Pain is part and parcel of the experience. That is why the pleasure is all the greater when things are brought to an end. When I copy the last page, I will simply close the book, and this work will exist solely in my manuscript. Who could reproach me then for adding my name above the title?

6. Noble Library

A noble library is much like a stomach. Strict attention must be paid to what goes into it. Only proper and fitting items should be allowed to enter a noble library. Should a book that doesn't belong find its way into such a place, it would be just like recklessly swallowing something unfit for consumption. Nausea and disgust would result. Those were my exact feelings upon entering the study and finding a book in my library that I had not put there. I felt a revulsion so strong that it completely supplanted the natural question as to how the book had got there. In the same vein, the first thoughts of a man whose stomach contains something improper will not be how it got there, but rather how to be rid of it. Health is, after all, more important than sheer intellectual curiosity.

I took hold of the book with two fingers and pulled it out. It certainly did not belong there, above all else because of its size. That's how it had caught my eye on the crowded bookshelf that covers one whole wall of my study. I've always felt the greatest possible disdain for paperback books. They are the ultimate profanation of an ideal that must remain exalted and noble at any cost. Only the ignorant and uninformed claim that a book should not be judged by its cover. Ostensibly, a great work remains a great work regardless of its packaging. Nonsense! Packaging must mirror the contents. Would you wrap a luxury item in old newspapers, for example? And what is a great work of literature if not the most luxurious of all items!

I didn't let the title deceive me. The title would have suited a deluxe edition, leather-bound, with gold lettering; it seemed almost sacrilegious on the ordinary plasticized cardboard of a paperback. But, then, the people who make paperbacks are known to be unscrupulous. Nothing is sacred to them. They will not hold back from using the most sublime words if they believe it will make them a profit. All they care about is money. I truly don't know where we'll end up if we keep on mis-using, trivializing and cheapening everything in this way.

Holding the object at arm's length, I walked briskly towards the kitchen. I stepped on the ped-al of the garbage can under the sink and opened my thumb and index finger. The paperback fell with a thud among the garbage where it belonged. I brushed my palms together. There! One must not be thin-skinned in such situations, but resolute and harsh. The treatment should be the same as for vermin. Like bedbugs or cockroaches. One must brook no quarter.

I returned to my study with a feeling of relief, but an unpleasant surprise awaited me. Although I had just thrown it away, the paperback book stood right where I'd found it a moment before: in my library! Blood rushed to my face. What was the meaning of this? Straight from the garbage to the bookshelf? The book was not only where it didn't belong—it had messed up and contaminated everything else around it. How awful!

This time I threw caution to the wind. I grabbed hold of the intruder and plucked it out, disrupting as I did so the impeccable order of the bona fide books surrounding it. I am always irritable when my bookshelves are out of alignment, but that could wait. I had to take care of this interloper, once and for all. I didn't hesitate for a moment. I opened the book approximately in half and did something I have never done before: I tore it in two. This, however, failed to quell the anger inside me—on the contrary—so I continued to tear it with undiminished vehemence.

Soon torn up and discarded pages were strewn all over the rug. Under other circumstances, this would have horrified me, but now it only increased my fury. Completely out of control, I sat on the floor and started tearing up the pages into tiny pieces. Almost confetti. I didn't stop until the last page had met the same fate. When nothing was left upon which to vent my rage, I finally calmed down.

Looking around at the scattered bits of paper, I was ashamed of what I'd done. Such an outburst of anger was highly uncharacteristic of me. But, worse yet, as I'd vented my frustration I'd felt enormous pleasure, almost delight. I had to ask myself if I'd lost my mind. All right, I'd been offended and provoked; it might even be said that a great injustice had been done to me, but even so. A man must restrain himself, after all. What would we come to if we gave free rein to our darkest impulses?

In addition, I had made a terrible mess, I who was so proud, even inordinately so, of my own neatness. I sighed and got up off the floor. I went to the closet in the vestibule, took out the vacuum cleaner and returned to the study. I spent a long time cleaning it thoroughly, as if the machine could suck up the invisible traces of my bad behavior along with the tiny pieces of paper. The vacuum cleaner became quite overheated before I finally turned it off. I detached the hose, put it all back in the closet and then went into the bathroom to take a shower, since I'd broken into a sweat.

I emerged refreshed and calm. I'd been through an unpleasant experience, but at least it was over now. The best thing would have been simply to forget the whole matter. Why obsess over how the book had gotten there? I couldn't care less. The knowledge would only burden me unnecessarily— and I couldn't exclude the possibility that I would not find an answer. In any case, now that I had most certainly rid myself of the annoying book, it no longer mattered.

My hopes, however, were premature. One glance at the bookshelf from the door to my study was all it took to realize that my troubles had just begun. As though mocking me, there, between two precious old tomes, stood the paperback, wholly untouched. My face flushed once again. I closed my eyes and took a deep breath, nodding slowly.

At first it seemed I was losing control of myself again. But the thought of what I might do were I once more to be blinded by rage helped me keep the upper hand. Blindness would not be a good ally here. I had to keep cool. I'd tried force and it hadn't worked. Now I had to try something more sophisticated. I had to plan things out. If you can't beat your enemy, try to outsmart him.

I was, unfortunately, completely inexperienced in this regard. Never once had I faced the challenge of getting rid of any books. Until then I had only tried to acquire them, something I'd become skilled at over time, as evidenced by my library. How was I to get rid of a book? And no ordinary book; rather, one that persistently refused to disappear, one that defied me with its insolence. I sat in the armchair facing the bookshelf and stared at the thin, short spine of the intruder. I began to draw the fingers of my left hand across my brow, as I always do when in deep thought.

Before long, an unusual comparison crossed my mind. I would be having this same trouble if I'd decided to kill myself. I wouldn't know exactly what to do in such circumstances, either. Although it might not appear so, I don't believe it's an easy thing to take your own life. But at least I would have at my disposal the diverse and abundant experience of previous suicides. Particularly the successful ones. Maybe I could use one of their methods on the paperback book.

I liked this idea. It sounded promising. All that remained was to choose the method. Taking stock of the several possibilities that popped into my mind, I decided that drowning would be the most appropriate. If I had decided to commit suicide, I would have chosen drowning. Particularly because there's no blood. I have an absolute horror of blood. In addition, the act of dying itself takes place under the surface and not before eye-witnesses, so no one suffers any shock on your behalf. Finally, there's a certain element of romanticism in it. Many great loves in literature have ended by jumping into the water.

Of the two things I needed for the drowning, one I had at home. I went to the pantry, opened the large cardboard box where I keep tools and various supplies, and took out a large ball of twine. The twine was thin and thus could not be used on myself, but would be more than sufficient for the wretched little book. I cut off more than I needed, just in case.

I had to go outside to find the other item I needed, although I wasn't quite sure where to look for it. Indeed, where can a man find a large rock in the middle of a city? I certainly could not break off a piece of the pavement or the facade of some building. The only place I might find a rock was the park, so that's where I headed. Before that, I put the book and twine in a large travel bag. They could have fit in my pocket, but I would need the bag for the rock. Walking through the streets with a huge rock in my hands would have been ridiculous. I would undoubtedly arouse suspicion among the passersby.

Finding a rock in the park was no easy matter. There were far fewer candidates than expected, and I had to find the proper moment to take one without being noticed. In the middle of a stretch of lawn lay a round flowerbed surrounded by pieces of chipped stone, half buried in the ground. I had to wait until there was no one nearby, which took quite some time, and then expended considerable effort in pulling one out. I had no time to clean the dirt off the bottom half. I quickly put it in my bag and moved away, leaving a hole in the stone ring similar to the hole left by an extracted tooth.

I was out of breath by the time I reached the bridge. The rock was considerably heavier than it looked; I had to carry the bag under my arm, not by the handle. I headed for the middle of the bridge because the water under that part was the deepest and fastest. Whatever sank there had no chance of surfacing. It turned out, however, that fulfilling my intention was no easy matter. Passersby were scarce, but there were many cars, including occasional police cars. I had to appear as inconspicuous as possible.

Turning towards the railing, I squatted down and took the rock out of the bag. I hoped no one could make out what I was doing from the road. Seeing me in that position, they would probably think I was an oddball or a drunk, but not a suicide. In any case, people in cars rarely care about what's happening outside. I tied one end of the twine firmly around the rock and the other end around the book.

Then I stood up and put the rock on the top of the railing. I didn't drop it right away. I stood there motionless for some time, pretending to be a stroller who had stopped briefly to enjoy the view from the bridge. Finally, when there seemed to be fewer cars, I pushed the rock and the book. They took longer to fall than I had expected, and the sound when they hit the water was considerably louder than I would have liked. Dragging the book after it like some sort of tail, the rock hit the surface flatly, producing an enormous splash.

If anyone had been on the bank around the bridge, my actions would have been detected. I quickly moved away from the spot so that no one would connect me with what had fallen. Once I'd put some distance behind me, fear was replaced by the feeling of relief and good spirits that befits a job well done. My hands were dirty from the earth, my coat as well, but I paid no attention to that. I had gotten rid of the book—that was all that mattered. Let it rest in peace amidst the mud at the bottom of the river.

But instead of being wherever the rock had pulled it, the book was waiting for me in my library upon my return. Not the least bit wet and muddy. On the contrary: clean and dry. When I saw it this time, however, I was not filled with anger as before. I only thought dully that things had gone too far. Everything has its measure, rudeness and impertinence as well. No paperback book could string me along like that. This had already become a question of honor.

As I cleaned myself up in the bathroom, I tried with the greatest composure to go through the other possibilities at my disposal. Jumping from a great height was also a favorite among suicides, and in literature. No small number of protagonists had sealed their fate in this way. There would be blood, of course, and eye-witnesses shocked at the none-too-pleasant sight, but this was unavoidable. My conscience was clear. I might have cause to reproach myself if I hadn't tried drowning first. I wasn't to blame for the failure of that scheme.

I didn't need to make any elaborate preparations to set in motion this new idea. I took the book off the shelf again and put on my coat, paying no attention to the fact that it was still wet. I might have dried it a little with a hair dryer, but I had run out of patience. This situation had to be resolved as soon as possible. It had already gotten on my nerves, something not at all advisable considering my high blood pressure.

I decided to climb to the top of the tallest building in town, not because a smaller building would not have served the purpose, but because it was the most suitable for the task at hand. There was a viewing deck at the top. When there wasn't much wind, like today, they let visitors go out onto it. A high wire fence surrounded the deck so that no one could accidentally or intentionally plunge from the precipice to his death over thirty floors below. If I'd been the suicide, I would have had a very difficult time, but things should have been easier for a paperback book.

The Library

I had my share of trouble nonetheless. The only person on the top of the building was a uniformed guard. If there had been other visitors and if my coat had not had a large stain down the front, he most likely would not have paid much attention to me. As it was, however, he kept his eyes glued on me, which was a serious hindrance. I spent twenty minutes or so walking along the fence pretending to look at the city panorama before I had a chance to spring into action.

Someone called the guard on his walkie-talkie; while he turned this way and that, trying to find the best position for reception, I whisked the book out of my pocket and tossed it over the fence. The man didn't notice a thing. I waited for him to finish his conversation, nodded to him briefly, giving a broad smile, and headed for the elevator. I was filled with elation and pride. It's no small thing to outwit a professional.

As I approached the ground floor, I imagined I would find a crowd of people around the fallen book. But there was nothing of the sort. The street bustled with people going about their business. What terrible indifference, I thought. Who cared about the fate of a book, even if it was only a paperback? Then I realized that I had accused the passersby unfairly. How could they show any compassion when there was no call for it? There was nothing anywhere near the spot where a book thrown off the viewing deck should have landed.

I went home, crushed by an evil foreboding that came true as soon as I entered my study. As before, the paperback book waited for me in the same place in my library. This stubbornness was truly shameful! It left me with no other choice. The time for handling the situation with kid gloves was over. There was a much more gory suicide than the ones I had already attempted. If it had suited an extremely refined literary heroine, I didn't see why it was out of place for the book. I removed the unseemly copy and headed straight for the train station.

I couldn't gain access to the platforms without a ticket, so I bought a ticket to the closest destination, although I wasn't going anywhere. I checked the schedule, found out where the next train would arrive, and went to that platform. I moved away from the passengers waiting for the train so there would be no witnesses. Some ten minutes later, a locomotive pulling a long line of cars started to enter the station. I let the first two cars go past, then turned my head away as I threw the book under the wheels of the third.

After the train had passed, I was briefly tempted to look at the rails, but I held back. I wouldn't have been able to stand the terrible sight: the completely mangled remains of the little book. Although it certainly deserved to disappear, I felt a certain sympathy for it. There had been no need for this to happen, but the book itself was to blame. In any case, it was all over now. There was no reason for me to stay there any longer. I would only appear suspicious.

This time upon arriving home, I wasn't even surprised when I found the paperback book where it certainly had no right to be. And in perfect shape. Not a hair missing from its head. What else could I have expected? I would have been amazed, in fact, had it been otherwise. My previously kind thoughts were replaced by deepest loathing. I couldn't look at it anymore. It was not worthy of being in the same room with me.

Not knowing what else to do, I headed for the kitchen to fix something to eat. This dashing around because of the book had kept me from eating all day long. My stomach growled and hunger pains prevented me from thinking properly about what I should do next. I put the cloth on the table and laid down a plate, knife, fork, spoon and linen napkin, then opened the refrigerator. The choices were rather meagre, however: a piece of dry cheese, a partially eaten sausage, half a jar of mustard and two lemons. It was clearly time to go to the store.

As I was closing the refrigerator, an idea came to me. I didn't take it seriously at first. Nonsense crosses my mind from time to time, as I suppose it does everyone's. I tried to drive it away, as I always do in such circumstances, but it refused to go. The longer it stayed with me, the less outlandish it seemed. Finally, I realized I had found the only real solution to my problem. I felt like slapping myself on the forehead. Of course! Why hadn't I thought of it before?

I went to my study, took the paperback book off the shelf and returned to the kitchen. I put it on a plate, sat down and tucked the napkin under my chin. First, I removed the cover with the knife and fork, as I would with a shell or wrapping. What was written on it promised true enjoyment, but one could certainly not rely on the honesty of whoever had produced it. Who knew what kind of a can of worms might be hiding behind the praiseworthy title *The Library*.

I could see by the table of contents that the book consisted of six parts. I assumed that each one had a different taste, so it was not advisable to eat them at the same time. I cut out each piece separately. Before commencing my meal, I wondered whether to add any spices. I looked at both sides of the cover, hoping to find some sort of instructions or advice in this regard, but since I found nothing, I decided not to try any experiments lest I spoil things. In the same vein, not knowing which drink would be most appropriate, I decided in favor of plain water. I couldn't go wrong there.

'Virtual Library' was quite reminiscent of a good Russian salad. It might have contained a bit more mayonnaise than suited my liking, though.

The Library

'Home Library' was like a thick, hearty beef soup with noodles. It seemed too hot, so I blew on the spoon. 'Night Library' corresponded to stuffed peppers. They contained the right proportion of meat and rice, which is very important for that dish. 'Infernal Library' was an excellent cherry pie. I don't really care for dessert, but this was an exception. 'Smallest Library' brought coffee with cream. I would have preferred something lighter, but one shouldn't be too picky.

I didn't know what could possibly follow this, but there was one more piece of the paperback on my plate: 'Noble Library.' Although already full, I didn't want to leave anything uneaten, and I was intrigued by it. I put a small bite cautiously into my mouth and started to chew. The taste seemed vaguely familiar, though I couldn't tell whether it was mostly savory, piquant, sweet or sour. It seemed to be all of these at the same time.

I continued eating, striving to figure it out. I was certain I'd tried it somewhere before. I liked it, perhaps more than all the rest. When I had swallowed the last piece, the pleasure that filled me was impaired somewhat by the fact that I could not recognize what I had eaten. But I didn't let this slight dissatisfaction spoil my good mood. I had accomplished my purpose. Not a crumb of *The Library* remained on my plate.

I got up from the table and headed towards my study. I felt not the slightest dread as to what I would find there. The paperback book might have been able to return from all the other places, but not from its current location. Its presence inside me was more than certain. I opened the door wide and smiled triumphantly at what my eyes beheld. The ugly intruder no longer sullied my noble library.

About the author

Zoran Živković was born in Belgrade, former Yugoslavia, in 1948. Currently a professor of creative writing at the University of Belgrade, he is the author of 18 books of fiction and five books of nonfiction. His writing belongs to the middle European *fantastika* tradition, exploring themes shared with such masters as Franz Kafka, Stanislaw Lem, Jorge Luis Borges and Abe Kōbō. He has won the World Fantasy Award, Miloš Crnjanski Award, Isidora Sekulić Award and Stefan Mitrov Ljubiša Award for lifetime achievement in literature, as well as being a runner-up for honors including the International IMPAC Dublin Literary Award (multiple times), the Shirley Jackson Award and the NIN Award.

He lives in Belgrade, Serbia, with his wife Mia, their twin sons Uroš and Andreja, and their three cats.

The Library

Works:

1. The Fourth Circle (1993)

2. Time-Gifts (1997)

3. The Writer (1998)

4. The Book (1999)

5. Impossible Encounters (2000)

6. Seven Touches of Music (2001)

7. The Library (2002)

8. Steps Through the Mist (2003)

9. Hidden Camera (2003)

10. Compartments (2004)

11. Four Stories Till the End (2004)

12. Twelve Collections and the Teashop (2005)

13. The Bridge (2006)

14. Miss Tamara, the Reader (2006)

15. Amarcord (2007)

16. The Last Book (2007)

17. Escher's Loops (2008)

18. The Ghostwriter (2009)

CPSIA information can be obtained
at www.ICGtesting.com
Printed in the USA
BVOW09s1117120717
489161BV00001B/15/P